The Death of the King's Canary

The Death of the
KING'S CANARY

DYLAN THOMAS
and
JOHN DAVENPORT

With an introduction by
Constantine FitzGibbon

HUTCHINSON OF LONDON

Hutchinson & Co (Publishers) Ltd
3 Fitzroy Square, London W1

London Melbourne Sydney Auckland
Wellington Johannesburg and agencies
throughout the world

First published 1976
© The estates of Dylan Thomas
and John Davenport 1976

Introduction © Constantine
FitzGibbon 1976

The publishers wish to thank
Miss Diana Davenport for her help in the
publication of this novel

Set in Monotype Fournier

Printed in Great Britain by
The Anchor Press Ltd and bound by
Wm Brendon & Son Ltd
both of Tiptree, Essex

ISBN 0 09 127510 5

CONTENTS

INTRODUCTION

by Constantine FitzGibbon

IN 1930 the late Wyndham Lewis, that fine painter, writer and many years earlier editor of an iconoclastic periodical appropriately called *Blast*, published a sort of a novel entitled *The Apes of God*. Wyndham Lewis had a profound loathing of all that was accepted, all that was fashionable in the arts. His novel was a ferocious send-up, perhaps the first, of all that was *idées reçues* in Flaubert's words, among the advocates and practitioners of what, in the Twenties, was still 'modern art', the first perhaps that was not written, for the wrong reason, by some academician or academic. It is a very long, rather congested and very complex satire, many of the characters being then quite easily recognizable. Perhaps nobody reads it today. It was certainly read by Charles Fisher, and probably by Dylan Thomas, when they were both working on *The South Wales Evening Post* in 1932. Dylan Thomas was then in his 18th year, Fisher a little older. Charles Fisher was one of Dylan's closest Swansea 'friends of my youth', and it may be doubted whether he ever made such friendships once he had left Swansea, tentatively in 1933, soon enough permanently.

He went to London filled with ambition to be recognized as a fine poet. Through Victor Neuburg and, to a slightly lesser extent, through Pamela Hansford Johnson, he met precisely the sort of literary characters whom Lewis had parodied. But he kept in touch with Swansea friends and it is in a letter to Fisher in 1938 that the idea of *Murder of the King's Canary* (as he was then calling it) appears. He was urging Fisher to collaborate and suggesting a discussion. *The Canary* was to be 'a novel, the detective story to end detective stories, introducing blatantly every character and situation – an inevitable Chinaman, secret passages, etc. – that no respectable writer would dare use now, drag hundreds of red herrings, false clues, withheld evidences into the story, falsify every issue, make many chapters deliberate parodies, full of clichés, of other detective writers'. A few months later he wrote again urging that he and Fisher 'must get started'.

Fisher, in fact, did produce a rough draft of a first chapter, but this bears no relation to Chapter One of the Thomas/Davenport text. It assembles and describes characters, unknown to that text, as a committee to choose a new Poet Laureate: and that is all. From that time on nothing seems to have been heard of the project until 1940. For by 1938 Dylan was already a famous, some would have said a notorious, and highly impoverished poet and was concentrating on his poems and to a lesser extent on his short stories. Even in his poems he would mull over ideas for years, going back to old notebooks, re-writing juvenilia. Very few of his poems were not conceived, at least, before ever he left Swansea. As for his prose and drama, he was less interested. *Under Milk Wood* was first discussed with Richard Hughes in 1939, with myself in 1944 and was finished in 1953, only a few days before his death. This constant return to his adolescence or very early manhood was characteristic of all his work, but more so in his prose even than in his verse. John Davenport once described him to me as the 'laziest intellect' he had ever known. Abstract ideas were of no interest to him at all. I once asked him a question about 'poetry', to which I received the very true answer: he was not interested in poetry, only in poems. He thus lacked the basic, almost ideological, venom that had led Wyndham Lewis to write *The Apes of God*. He was however a fine parodist of other men's poems.

In the dreadful, and to him terrifying, summer of 1940 he was staying with John Davenport. I knew John Davenport well, and would like to pay public tribute here to an old friend, a generous, difficult, brilliant man with a very fine and profound knowledge of the arts, of all the arts, a consummate pianist, a collector of great paintings by artists then still unknown, and when an undergraduate a poet compared by his contemporaries in the very early thirties to Auden and Spender and Day Lewis. Yet he, too, dried up. He went to see T. S. Eliot. He told me that Eliot had advised him to write nothing for ten years, and that he had never forgiven Eliot this bad advice, for he never wrote again. He made a certain amount of money from films, and in 1940 was able to support the Thomas family in his comfortable English country house. When he was rich, his money was yours, when he was poor, yours was his.

John Davenport was an unusually strong man, quite short but almost square, at one time a very good heavyweight boxer. In literature he was a perfectionist, and this was his emotional downfall, for he could not, ten years after his perhaps apocryphal conversation with T. S. Eliot, ever achieve his own standards. I once stopped him from throttling Dylan – true, it was very late at night – for the very simple and expressed reason that Dylan was a *poet* and John was not.

In 1940 Dylan revived the idea for *The King's Canary* and on this book he and Davenport collaborated. It was intended to be a good joke, and to make money, but of course was quite unpublishable while the main characters were alive. Dylan Thomas maintained that Davenport had written most of the verse parodies. This may well be untrue, for if Dylan was not proud of them, he would have given their authorship to John. Others have said that their skill is far beyond what were Davenport's capacities. Some of the prose, but not a great deal, shows evidence of Dylan's verbal pyrotechnics. Apparently they collaborated in a room that John Davenport had fixed up as a model of an old-fashioned pub, complete with barrels of beer, while Caitlin danced in a distant summerhouse to the music of a portable gramophone.

Very frequently I receive letters from post-graduate students asking for help in their Ph.D. theses concerning the late Dylan Thomas. Here, I can give no help. On the other hand, I feel that a most useful Ph.D. thesis might be based upon this book. A subtle scholar could devote a great deal of his time to speculation as to who wrote what in this curious book. But then Dylan Thomas also announced, as part of his policy towards the world: 'Bewilder 'em.'

CHAPTER ONE

CHOOSING THE CANARY

His nerves had not been soothed by the bishop's unctuous platitudes. An unsettling evening. First, the bomb in the shrubbery – no loss of life, but such a *noise*; then dinner, and he had looked forward to dinner – every bottle of the Chambertin 1911 hopelessly grey-haired. Only to be expected, perhaps, but a disappointment. Then the bishop. Thank God he'd gone to bed at last, taking their memories with him. It was only when the bishop came that the Prime Minister realized how dull his life had been.

The door behind him opened. What were they going to do to him now? It was his private secretary. The Prime Minister looked relieved: he knew that he had nothing to fear. Peace reigned temporarily on earth and peace would reign at Chequers.

'Thought you'd gone to bed.'

'Just on my way, sir. I've brought you the poets.'

What midnight delegation of poets had tracked him here?

'The poets?'

'For the Laureateship, sir. You said you'd decide this weekend. I've made a few notes about their background and so on.'

'Have I *got* to read them, Faraday?'

'Afraid so, sir.'

'Well, leave them on the table. Goodnight.'

'Goodnight, sir.'

His condor's head caught the lamplight as he left the library. A profound self-compassion filled the Prime

Minister. He rang the bell; and, crossing the room, chose a cigar.

'You rang, sir?'

He hated the butler's great slab of a face.

'A bottle of the Napoleon brandy, Bibby.'

'Very good, sir.'

The cigar was drawing well. He crossed to the window and listened conscientiously to the nightingales until the brandy came.

'You needn't wait up, Jackson.'

'Thank you, sir. Goodnight, sir.'

'Goodnight.'

The butler, whose name was Philpot, closed the door behind him. What with a new Prime Minister every month, it was no wonder the old muddleheads got mixed up.

He poured the brandy into the rummer and inhaled. Slowly the night received him again, a kind island between the days. *People*. How he hated people! Almost as much as he liked things. His eye fell on the pile of brightly wrapped poets, and he sighed. Ah well, perhaps it might not be so ghastly a task, after all: he did not read much English poetry later than Pope, although he admired Tennyson's ear. These people might be interesting.

On top of the books lay a page in Faraday's neat script.

'Albert Ponting, born Balham, 1910. Ed. privately. Did Chemistry course at Polytechnic. *Must read*, but suggest unsuitable.'

The Prime Minister picked up a volume called *Claustrophosexannal*. The title was puzzling. He opened the book and began to read.

LAMENTABLE ODE

BY ALBERT PONTING

I, I, my own gauze phantom am,
My head frothing under my arm,
The buttocks of Venus for my huge davenport.
I orgillous turn, burn, churn,
As his rubbery bosom curds my perspiring arm –
The gust of my ghost, I mean –
And he wears no woman-sick, puce, and oriflammed a brow
That, yes, yes, my hair screamed aloud
Louder than death's orchestra or sirocco.
The urge of the purge of the womb of the worm
I renege in the flail-like failing of
The detumescent sun.
This my crepuscular palimpsest is:
I am so greatly him that lazarhouses and such
Lascivious lodges of the unloved
Peel like pomegranates at my nasal touch
And Balham faints in a scalecophidian void.
To him who broods in the nests of my arches,
Fallen or Charing Cross's, like a big bumbling bird,
Before the metropolitan horde
Funicling darkly lairward
I lay the most holy gifts of my spilt flesh:
Far beyond comprehension of golden asinine error
I raise to the mirror the maggots and lumps of my terror.

He glanced again at his secretary's notes, and raised his
eyebrows. He had once been Minister of Education, and
was still keenly interested in all educational questions.
'Privately' sounded fishy, but the Polytechnic, with its
reputation for accuracy – empirical tests were a favourite
with the Prime Minister – might have spared him this
shock. What on earth was a davenport? He walked over to
the shelves; and discovered that in English it was an

3

escritoire and in American a settee. It did not seem to clear up the line. He had never been in Balham, and the poem was not enlightening. He glanced through the rest of the book, his eye sliding distastefully from adjective to adjective; but the humourless self-absorption and the faulty syntax of the writer soon defeated him. He drank, poured again, and reached for another book.

Faraday had written:

'Fergus O'Hara, *né* Solomon, b. London 1899, resident N. Ireland (Belfast). Suggest not, but politically OK.'

Faraday liked to relieve his donnishness with an occasional transatlantic phrase. The Prime Minister opened the volume which was called *The Winter Awakening*. The first poem was an Elegy.

ELEGY

BY FERGUS O'HARA

The Fool would call to the Metal Man
And get him no reply;
The Bone would bleach by Rosses Point,
The Hawk fall from the sky,
The Rose wither; and I
Would take my way to Drumcliff Cross
And stand by an empty grave;
And with me a girl with milk-white arms
Fair as the ghost of Maeve
Herself pure as a wave.
And all the lights of Sligo Town
Would fail and would wax dim,
And their fall would be filled with the flying
Of the swan which would be him
Sailing over the evening's rim.
I would hearken and I would hear
The voice of the dying swan
Saying 'I who have loved a thousand loves,

> *Each of them pale and wan*
> *As the moon over Conn,*
> *Am come winging back from exile*
> *From the land of Villon's ghost*
> *Westwards over the grave of Blake*
> *To the love I loved the most.*
> *Not that I would boast.*
> *To Sligo I go, and in Drumcliff*
> *At last shall the Bone be laid*
> *And the Hawk shall be flying above me*
> *And the Fool's cap in that glade;*
> *And the Rose shall give me shade.*
> *No more shall come lust from Byzantium*
> *To torture the calm of Coole.*
> *Though in Gort there will be much keening,*
> *And a Tower fall in Kinnoull,*
> *Quiet will lie the Fool.'*

This time he was genuinely upset. How repellent the easy vulgarity of the writing and the knowing use of place names! Yeats was one of the few contemporaries he read; he wondered if many of those artificial flowers had been flung at the empty grave. No, decidedly not this incompetent Baedeker.

He walked over to the open window, glass in hand, thinking of great men dead and little men living. Outside, the night was mercifully still, in spite of the glugging of the poetical birds. Sometimes they set the teeth on edge, like slate pencils. However, they weren't people.

Comforted, he picked up the next on the pile. He was glad to notice that the title was simply *Poems*. By Robert Gordon. What had Faraday got to say about Gordon? 'B. Edinburgh 1903. Ed. Loretto and Balliol. Sound man, *but American wife*. Formerly lecturer in Tennessee. Scarcely suitable.'

The first poem was called 'The Two Journeymen'.

5

THE TWO JOURNEYMEN

Going out, for a small grail, two men of words and straw,
The first sickly and rich, the second most wild and poor,
And both of them tall and rotten as a brothel door,

Upped and girded their parchment gaiters on four weak legs,
Covered in ink and quills their heads the colour of eggs,
And mounted at the papery gates two great stone dogs.

It was on a very strange journey our heroes galloped,
Two weirdly talking rompers they feebly larruped,
And the birds who told verses over their shoulders chirruped.

Resembling, I hear, two hay-wisps riding on horses
They, trembling, drove through the terrible of Courses
And each in his sweet turn fell to the strangest forces,

Armies of images, fabulous campers and sutlers,
Sailors from drunken boats with hiccup and gold cutlass,
Frogs with bad flowers and metaphors big as Atlas,

Thin tin words doing little in helmets but scrape and blow,
Frond and shard and frieze and calyx crying Io,
More poems than I could number making a brassy show.

First one then the other, ambushed by words with a knife,
A rose, a wet sponge, a grim tractor, lisped for his life,
But splinth and jacinth, kestrel and neon, they widowed a wife.

Like unto ghosts of straws, see on long dogs how they creep
Through pastoral dead groves counting the ode-worried sheep:
O, O ambrosia and nightingale wound them too deep.

King Christ save their souls as riding dry hillock and heath
They chanced on a land railed around with bare truths and teeth
Where even the graves were made empty and there blew not one
wind's breath.

Where the moon was exactly moon and nothing was growing
Is, Was and no adjectives laid them fatally groaning,
And, 'How you both happened is death,' said the Great Unpoem.

The Prime Minister rather liked it, in spite of the obscurity. It sounded as though it were about to break into sense at any moment, and perhaps it might make sense to someone who lived more in the world than himself, or at any rate who had visited Tennessee.

The other poems baffled him, too; he took some more brandy and turned to *Midsummer Eclogues* by Edmund Bell. 'Edmund Bell. B. Taunton, 1888.' Wrote Faraday. 'Ed. locally. Exeter College, Oxford. Excellent war record. *V. strong candidate.*' That sounded all right. He opened the volume at 'The Wayfaring Tree'.

THE WAYFARING TREE
BY EDMUND BELL

Lithewort, some call thee, or Old Cottoner;
Coventree, some, or Twistwood; Mealytree;
Whitewood, or Lithy-one, or Wayfarer;
  Whipcrop, to me.

Good Gerarde first, and, later, Parkinson
Noted thy fondness for the roadside hedge
Or thicket; and we find, wherever Chalk,
  Thee, for a pledge;

In Winter shewing thy large naked buds,
All rough with starry hairs (which keep off Frost,
As do the Chestnut's varnish and tough scales)
  Bravely up-tossed.

And in the Summer thy broad hirsute leaves
Looking as dusty as a miller's coat
– Above them spreading round white heads of flowers –
  Airily float.

Thy downy stems are never very stout;
But branchy, and with wrinkled heart-shaped leaves,
Blunt-ended, white beneath; edges sharp-toothed
  As ancient reeves.

First red, then black, thou flower'st in May and June;
Five-lobed your clusters, and the stamens five
Extrude from mouth – corollas funnel-shaped,
　　　Sweetly alive.

Here, sitting beside the seasonable fire,
I watch the smoke curl blue from my last pipe,
Whose stem is fashioned from thy year-old shoot,
　　　Severed ere ripe.

Himself no botanist, he felt the authenticity of the poem. This fellow knew what he was talking about, and there was a certain mellowness in the writing not altogether unpleasing. He turned the pages, and read a poem describing the nesting habits of the crested grebe; a third about preparing ground bait; and, at last, a very long one, called 'The Water Diviner'. Good though they were in their way, they never seemed to move far from the village pump; and although abstractions were welcome by their absence, a Poet Laureate should surely be able to leave the ground now and again. This chap was positively buried in it, a veritable mole. He put the book on one side for further consideration, and took a little more brandy. He felt tolerant and benign.

A light shone through the window, and flickered round the room.

'Very sorry, sir, thought you'd gone to bed. I saw the reflection of the light and . . .'

'That's all right, Philpot. Goodnight.'

'Goodnight, sir.' And Jackson the nightwatchman disappeared into the darkness. Funny thing, he thought, that the Prime Minister shouldn't bother about the blackout. Still, he ought to know. After the second Great War blackouts remained general even during 'Peace'. But there was a good deal of slackness.

Lighting another cigar, the Prime Minister chose a

volume called *Look, Dead Man*. The writer's name was Wyndham Snowden. His dossier read: 'Wyndham Nils Snowden. B. London, 1904. Ed. Westminster and Christ Church. Very popular with the younger men. But *a bit of a red.*'

The poems seemed to consist of a series of conversations; or rather, a series of lectures. They were all addressed to other, dead, writers. There was a long squabble with a tongue-tied Spenser in the metre of the *Faerie Queene*; a rap on the knuckles for Scott in the metre of *Marmion*. The one which he read through first was called 'Brothers Beneath the Skin'.

BROTHERS BENEATH THE SKIN

Preached the archbishop from his high gothic pulpit
After the choirboys' shrilling and the canons' Oxford roar;
>*'England Home and Beauty*
>*Are for those who do their Duty,*
Respect the King, respect the Cloth, give honour to the Law.'

The communist made answer from his back room in Bloomsbury,
Marx and Lenin open by the Woodbines on the floor:
>*'You may preach of Kingdom Come*
>*But in factory and slum*
Is brewing such a trouble as was never seen before.'

Then cried the tired mechanic with the good bones mechanically,
'O I am fine and dandy and the master of my soul.
>*My granddad was a peasant*
>*And it wasn't very pleasant*
Without cinemas and birth-control and unions and the dole.'

Arrogant in answer spoke the massive humming turbines
Turning in the powerhouse like the grinding mills of God:
>*'Little man in your manhole*
>*You may stand at the control*
But you're no more our master than a peasant with a hod.'

9

Cool in his clinic chimed the sexless psychoanalyst:
'You may flap your little flags and build Empires overseas
        But there's something lies behind
        In the bad rooms of your mind
Made of father-hates, castration-fears, and such-like things as
                                these.

Hotly they answered from their battleships and compounds,
Plethoric, bristling, turning red and white and blue:
        'You nasty little cad,
           We've clean bodies; and, by Gad,
We'd rather have a dirty mind than be a filthy Jew.'

Thus said the poet in the prep room with his pretty ones,
Calling pukka sahibs and the soakers on verandahs:
        'Lo! the true-blue day has scrammed
           When you Did and Iffed and Damned,
And all the jellybellies are as soft as baby pandas.'

Lightning-quick as Larwood cried the silly, silly cricketers:
'Dirty little highbrow with your black and bitten nails,
        We knew the Empire backwards
        When you were learning sex words
And the lesser breeds of scribblers were hanging by their tails.'

Straight-mouthed the master, eternally quadrangular:
'Oh purple men at tiffin with your horse-faced better halves,
        Did you never stop to think
        As you downed the sun in drink
That the bums you bruise and beat will have the last and longer
                               laughs.'

'Look what we have given them: God, and guns and discipline,
Syphilis and alcohol, and missionaries and whips.'
        Came the cry beyond the waves
        Of emancipated slaves:
'We were doing very nicely till the white lord came in ships.'

'You have stole my Chantey metre,' called Kipling from the clouds,
'And what you've written in it ain't no bleedin' earthly good;

> *You're a lily-livered pup*
> *What should be delivered up*
> *To do packdrill with the Horse Marines and Foot, which same*
> > *are rude.'*

> *Look, dead man, at this Empire, at this Eastscape of suffering,*
> *Monocled glaucoma over India's coral strand.*
> > *They can hear in twilight Ealing*
> > *The forts fall in Darjeeling*
> *As the last White Hope is snuffed out in that dark-skinned*
> > *No-Man's-land.*

It did not seem in very good taste or even true. Perhaps 'the younger men' didn't bother to know anything about the systems they attacked. Of course, Kipling had kicked up his heels a bit when he was young; but then the Prime Minister had never greatly cared for Kipling. Such a noisy, knowing little man. Probably Mr Snowden was, too. He placed the book firmly on the rejected heap, and picked up the next, a very slim volume bound in imitation vellum.

'Sigismund Gold, *né* Goldstein. B. Birmingham 1880. Ed. Birmingham Grammar School and Downing College, Cambridge. Clerk in War Office. Safe but Jewish.'

BEAUTY
BY SIGISMUND GOLD

> *All that is beauty*
> > *in so small a space*
> *earth, sea and sky*
> > *in your upturned face*

> *Troy and Byzantium*
> > *and far Cathay*
> *Carthage and Hellas*
> > *in mortal clay*

Roses and gillyflowers
lilies and rue
chrysanthemums, orchids
all sprout in you

Arcturus and Sirius
shine in your eyes
you have stolen their lamps
and defrauded the skies

Helen, and Thetis
and fair Heloise
you are more perfect
than any of these

The past and the future
combine in the now
and immortality
gleams on your brow

Yet you must perish
and fall in the dust
as all that is beauty
eventually must.

Here at least he knew where he was. This was bad, very bad. Some of the poems were Greekish and some of them were Irish and some of them were suburban. They were never Jewish or Birmingham or indiscreet, though an occasional 'Epigrammatic' (shorter) poem would gently and obviously score off some unpopular public figure. The writer's books seemed to sell in large quantities, he noticed, but his conscience really would not let him put the book on one side. 'There's a limit,' he said out loud, quite angrily. 'There is, dammit, a limit.'

The brandy sank in the bottle. His eyes closed, he sniffed at the rummer, cherishing it in his hand. He opened his left eye and focussed on a Ming horse about four yards away.

Then the right eye. Not so clear. He put his eyeglass into the right eye and looked again. Better. Now the left eye again. Opening and closing his eyes alternately he made the little horse move backwards and forwards. The Prime Minister giggled. Then turned once more to his task. *The Inward Heart*, this one was called, by Christopher Garvin.

'Christopher Garvin. B. London, 1908, son of Lt General Sir Herbert Garvin. Ed. Winchester and New College. *Bit of a red*. Risky.'

He remembered the last 'red'. What did red mean? Surely that adolescent indignation wasn't so very alarming? The poems were full of gasworks and power stations, and bewildered boys. A typical one was called 'Parachutist'.

PARACHUTIST

I shall never forget his blue eye,
Bright as a bird's but larger,
Imprinting on my own
Tear-wounded but merciless iris
The eternal letters
Of his blond incomprehension.

He came down lightly by the lilypool
Where a bird was washing,
But he did not frighten her:
A tousselled boy from the skies
Petrol should not have signed
Shamefully to his surprised dishonour;
His uniform like an obscene shroud
Fretted his hands that should have held in peace
A girl's two kind ones in a public park,
Handled a boat or fashioned simple things,
Flutes, clogs, and little wooden bears,
Or in beer gardens by the ribboning Rhine
Mirthfully gestured under linden trees.

Now these once loving-kindly hands
Cherished, like an adder picked up on a walk,
A tommy gun, cold threat to love in steel:
Icarus he stands; his silken clouds of glory
Trailing behind him — a bird's broken wing —
Still trembling from his fallen angel's flight
Down the sky weeping death.

His wide amazed gaze like the child Mozart's
Straight would have stripped like an x-ray
Each last layer of my inmost heart
Had he but seen his enemy standing there
By the desk heaped high with betrayals and public faces
Of private friends false as a walking tour.

Suddenly splintered like glass the brittle dome
Enfolding our silence; an unjust bullet
Destroyed the delicate whorl on whorl of his brain.
Under the rosebush his trigger finger trembled.

O young man; O my might-have-been; understander.
We could have watched the dawn rise over München
Or gathered chestnuts under Hanniker Hill.
I who have known you only in unknowing
May now, alone, know you never at all,
O enemy not of my choice.

He finished reading it, and when he put it down, felt quite sorry for the boy. Must be pretty bad having Garvin for a father, the pompous bully. Still, it would hardly do. He began to wonder if England would ever have another Laureate. Not that it would greatly matter, he thought, pouring from the bottle. It was a ridiculous appointment. 'A ridiculous appointment,' he enunciated aloud.

He was getting through the poets splendidly, knocking them over left and right. He opened the *Collected Poems* by John Lowell Atkins.

'J. L. Atkins. B. Boston, 1890. Ed. Harvard, Heidelberg

and Trinity, Cambridge. Naturalized 1917. *Very sound*, but I don't think quite right for the job.'

He had heard of Atkins. They were both honorary fellows of the same Oxford college, but had never met. At least it would be literate work, he supposed. He began to read.

WEST ABELARD

BY JOHN LOWELL ATKINS

1

Everything is the same. It only differs
in the subjective mind which is the same
being or not-being, born, unborn,
a wind among leaves deciduous or dead.
It does not matter where
it does not matter.
Windfall or wordfall or a linnet's feather
in rank orchards where perpetual turns the worm
It is not different: always is the same
Only the footsteps on the dusty stair
creak and are silent
only the footsteps
Quod idem peccatum non puniat Deus
hic et in futuro
Lord if I suffer now and not hereafter
if it be graver, Lord, to bear one's sin
than pay the fine of death at the time of lilacs
when wings and wind in the orchard ruin the blossom
Lord, if I suffer now?

2

sin solved in Death is quite consumed
(no absolution's without pain)
a death in life may be resumed
but sin unshriven must remain

Augustine fervent in belief
preferred to fight the flesh in men
than to obtain the false relief
whose advocate was Origen.

The body's urge is natural
acceptance of the bread and wine
proves Logos flesh, and so may all
the thinking beasts become divine

Abelard torn twixt God and lust
consumed by sense of sin unsolved
clouding the spirit in the dust
searched through the Fathers, unresolved

Fulbert crept up on priestly foot
quenched the hot fever in the bone
his knife struck at the problem's root:
Abelard lay at peace, alone.

3

Even the end is similar. It ends
and there's an end.
A whispering under the door, a weeping
in violet darkness when the last wheels are still.
And you
turning blind eyeballs to a sky of stone
praying you know not wherefore or
to whom.
Falling into the darkness into the grave
out of a darkness falling; being or not-being, man, unmanned,
it is not different.
It is not different and it is better
that so it should be.
Everything is the same.

He felt queerly depressed, and reached once more for the brandy. Not much left. The nightingales had sung themselves silent, and the room was cold. He went over to the window. No moon. A figure loomed up in the darkness.

'Who is that?' he called sharply.

'Only me, sir.'

'What on earth are you doing out there?'

'I'm assistant watchman tonight, sir. After that bomb . . .'

'Oh yes, of course.' The Prime Minister had quite forgotten about the bomb.

'Well, goodnight, Andrews.'

He wished the man had stayed. He felt in need of company. That *was* a lugubrious poem; and the trouble was that it was true. Everything *was* the same. Dull, too. But it would never do to tell them so. There were only three books left now. The first of these was called *All Honour and Glory* and was by Sir Frank Knight. He drank deeply before taking the plunge.

ALL HONOUR AND GLORY

BY SIR FRANK KNIGHT

One of the Western men, I, in this hour
Of England's direst need, whom beef and beer
Full nourished, and dozens of bottles of excellent port,
Who the kindly fens erst nursed when the heart's fires flamed
Full as a beacon in my generous youth,
I, I acclaim thee, sea-girt Mother of Fame!
Mind of an Englishman, not meanly planned,
Cramped by false wit or swol'n with sophistries,
But stuffed with dreams and ancient memory!
Brave thoughts come back of endless argument
With golden friends now dead or overseas;
Of wily trout lured from the streams of May,
And pheasants in October coming high;
Of willow-haunted fields – the leathern click
Of ball on bat and bail, while all the Yard

17

Echoed with clean applause; of silver nights
Falling on Oxford roofs, while mingled with the bells
The bitterns boomed, and all the rooks of Balliol
Filled the mind with a vast, an endless, surprise;
Of English dawns, plashy with English dew,
And English water-wagtails on English lawns,
And Englishmen walking in the English way
In England. . . .

No, no, no. This was too much. Really appalling. And how the brute would love the job! They were members of the same club, though scarcely on speaking terms. A drunken old bore, Knight borrowed and pontificated in an ever diminishing circle. He owed the Prime Minister a pound, having once (in the English way) laid a wager about the date of the present war which, being an uninformed and not very intelligent man, he had lost. The Prime Minister had an advantage, being, oddly enough, neither one nor the other; but he'd never received the pound, and only a fortnight before he'd had to pay for one of the Dreadful Knight's drinks. The would-be Poet Laureate was adept at such tricks. In this case, it lost him the job more certainly than his verse. Only two more!

Poems by William Dudley.

'William Dudley. Ed. Eton and King's.' That seemed all right. He put Faraday's note on one side and began to read.

REQUEST TO LEDA

Not your winged lust but his must now change suit.
The harp-waked Casanova rakes no range.
The worm is (pin-point) rational in the fruit.

Not girl for bird (gourd being man) breaks root.
Taking no plume for index in love's change
Not your winged lust but his must now change suit.

Desire is phosphorus: the chemic bruit
Lust bears like volts, who'll amplify, and strange
The worm is (pin-point) rational in the fruit.

Was it the brandy or was he losing his reason? He had always been terrified of going out of his mind. It had happened to so many of his colleagues. He concentrated hard, but it was no good: the rest of the poem was just as obscure. It looked clear enough, too. Dropping the book at his side he picked up the last volume. It was called *A Time To Laugh* and was by Hilary Byrd. He emptied the last drop of brandy into his glass, and drained it before he began. The book seemed to be a loosely connected narrative, using different poetic forms. A young man looking for a Leader. The Leader, when found, proved to be living at the top of a mountain. The final poem was called:

MANMOUNTAIN

This was my test: not by the easier route
But through the gentians and the rocks to hurl
My adolescence; the glacier bruised my foot
and I laughed despite at the icy wind's up-curl.
My goal was there, poised on the peak's white winter
As an eagle's eyrie breasting the burning blast,
And though the old world round me cruelly splinter
Not was for me in my pride to be downcast.

'Mountains,' he said, 'are only high in space:
Make the Andes your molehill and below
Map in the valleys lofty continents,
Plan power-houses for your island race.
Take a divining rod, and boldly throw
Alpenstock down; use plainsman arguments.'

This would do. It was frightful, but it would do. A sort of sonnet, but bringing in power-houses – 'striking a note of modernity throughout'. He hoped he might see Max in London. When they were sufficiently civilized, human beings were scarcely *people* at all. He felt that the stuff he'd been reading through the night wasn't likely to appeal to anybody except people. Well, he'd give them what they wanted. He steadied himself by the table, fumbled for Faraday's notes, which had fluttered to the floor.

'Hilary Byrd. B. 1907. Eton and Trinity. Son of Sir Austin Byrd. Airman. Possibility. Dymmock Hall, Suffolk.'

Possibility, indeed! Old Austin Byrd's son. Funny thing he should write poetry; but still, he was a poet; and he would be the next Poet Laureate!

He chuckled. This made the evening seem almost worthwhile.

Staggering slightly, he moved to the door, and, removing with some difficulty his shoes – he had once had a nasty tumble on the polished stairs – he climbed, still chuckling, up to bed.

Outside in the shrubbery the other bomb ticked softly. But it only killed a gardener. The Prime Minister slept heavily and undisturbed.

CHAPTER TWO

A GILDED CAGE

EVERYONE felt terrible at Dymmock Hall. It was noon on a bad day, the worst in a poor week, airless and drizzling, a mist over Suffolk, over Suffolk alone, as Ponting pretended to imagine, damping the hot June and making the people who trod water through it resemble fishes or ghosts or even – Ponting phrased in front of the mirror advertising Worthington – the ghosts of fishes. He was feeling creative and knew he could do nothing about it; images came with such ease to him as he carefully disarranged his hair and loosened his woollen tie that he knew he ought to suspect them. The window blind, half drawn, was a shadower of tortured destiny; the rain that just fell down was pecking the air; he undid a button of his tennis shirt, and the pale hairless flesh inside was an officious habiliment around ruin. Against his own criticism he wrote the three images down with an eyebrow pencil on the dressing-table cloth. Tortured destiny pecking the air around ruin. It was better than all Garvin.

He dropped the ash of his cigarette purposely on to the lapel of his blazer. 'Pecking the tortured air,' he said aloud to the tall, thin, very young man in the mirror, and waited, almost sincerely, for an answer. There were spots in front of his eyes. It was a consolation to think that there were, at that very moment – 'very moment,' replied the ghost in the mirror, showing the smoker's teeth, being Shelley and Irving at the same time but both a dim green – spots and worse, conventional mice, nausea faceted like diamonds – Ponting raised the eyebrow pencil and looked again at his friend and enemy and lover, Albert on glass – in front of the eyes of Christopher Garvin, Robert Cameron, and Magda Crawshay.

He was glad that the manservant had myopia. The manservant's name was Grant; Ponting would have been delighted when breakfast of Prairie Oyster and black coffee came on a tray, to call him General, but there was nobody to listen: Grant was deaf, too.

The hairbrushes on the dressing table were stiff with Brylcreem. Mother had forgotten to clean the clotted comb with a pin. The pyjamas on the floor had 'Albert' stitched on them in red cotton. His father's dinner jacket, too tight under the arms, came from Walton-on-Thames.

Blindness and deafness had their advantages. Grant would never see that his toothbrush and Colgate's were wrapped in the *News Chronicle*. The pulling down of a stray lock of wettened hair, the ordered rumpling of his dark flannels – Mother should never have put them under the mattress: poets were baggy – the settling of the cigarette he detested at the drooping corner of his mouth, a quick false smile to the figure in the pool of the mirror, 'Now for it', in quite an unaffected voice, and he was done. He was ready for his first Dymmock day.

Robert Gordon, wearing white flannels and a tie, knotted too loosely for a business man but still not aggressively the tie of a man opposed to business, decorated with pastelled cubist birds, stood before the mirror in the Royal Room – 'the room where the Queen slept,' his host had said, but no one knew which Queen or of what kind – and deprecated his worn, Scotch face and the bulrushes painted around the glass. On the wall near the mirror was written, in a cultivated hand, 'Flax 34092 is *my* number.'

He could not think why his face reminded him of Scotland. It was only a face, big-boned, hollow-eyed, much lined from the nose to the mouth, bushily eyebrowed, cautious-lipped; the detecting of national characteristics was a dull game; an eye, he had been taught to believe, was not a delicate gazelle, but a glassy ball in the top of the face through which one observed the antics of others; he refused to think of himself as a lump of clay shaped in a set country, by a mother from Fife, by a clerical father who believed in home rule and free will. He was Gordon the international breather, he was cosmopolitan Robert the normal man. But, staring into his own eyes, he began again to think of home rule and a detached house in the better quarter of Edinburgh, he saw Gordon R. in the school register and remembered with an almost pleasant agony the delights of cricket, a game he had never been able to play or enjoy.

'I'm Gordon in Dymmock,' he said aloud. He found the old parting in his hair and made it straight. Allowing himself one moment of absolute, drowning fancy, he saw great Gordon, the gentleman poet, all things to all men, a ferocious layer, a shrewd assessor, a fatal man but never too passionate, enter the luncheon-room to loud, brass music and cries of 'Why, look who's here!' 'Robert, me old cocksparrow. What's the latest on "Change"?' 'Sit here,' 'No, here,' 'There's a letter for you from W. B. Yeats, Laura Riding, Anthony Eden and the boys from the Crawford poker school.' Then he said, aloud again, 'Time for lunch. Come on. No nonsense.'

On the way to the door he stumbled over an occasional table, too short for practical use, and saw for the first time that it was shaped out of an elephant's member. Funny chap, young Byrd. No taste. Too much taste. It was all the same.

He marched down the stairs, stamping to give himself confidence, though each step jarred from coccyx to cervix.

On a refectory table in the hall he saw friendly bottles; and with the bottles, eggs and Worcester sauce and ice. He splashed ice and whiskey into a glass with a brave, shaking hand.

Cracking the ice between his jaws he mixed another drink and let his gaze wander more than three yards. All the way down the house he had been conscious only of buckskin shoes and bony hands. Now he looked round pluckily, the drink warming his lankiness. He drained the glass again and walked through the open door of the library, armed against eccentricity or beauty.

There was nobody in the library except a stranger behind *The Times*, and the black cat with such a whimsical name – Mrs Purry Wurry, he remembered, was her name before tea and what she was called after dinner he did not dare to think – that Hilary was the one man in the house who could talk to her without embarrassment.

Derek Gill said 'Good morning' shyly. He did not know Robert Gordon. Please God, he thought, he is not the poet who ate the barometer and drank the eau-de-cologne. It was difficult to tell who was who in Dymmock Hall, and all you could do was to hope for the best. This one looked like an under-secretary, but his tie was too big. Perhaps he was the actor. Oh, don't let him be Hamish Corbie. Perhaps he was a schoolmaster or a lawyer.

'Have you seen the news?' he asked. 'Burma's fallen.'

Gordon was taken aback. This decorous fellow, smoking at *The Times*, was unexpected. Screwed up to whiskey pitch, ready for the last Niagara of sophistication, and ready to crash over it in his simple tub, he was abashed by the acres of flat ground lying ahead. He dimly remembered the young man's appearance, but last night had been so confused.

'Know China at all?' he mumbled bluffly.

'No, but I used to work at the BM.'

'French friend of mine, archaeologist in Indo-China, said that the latest diggings . . .'

'I'm afraid I know very little about it.'

Gill felt that he was in a false position. He had arrived the night before, long after dinner, his car having broken down. It was always happening. At Amberley he had arrived a day late, though the Duke and Duchess hadn't seemed to mind. He sometimes wished he had a different job, yet it sounded so attractive when one talked about it. The architectural expert of *Hill and Dale*: what could be pleasanter? Long weekends in the greater or smaller country houses of England, and then a signed article filling in the spaces between Belton's excellent photographs. But the ambiguous position – half guest, half tripper-journalist – had never ceased to bother him; and Dymmock Hall promised to be a really trying job. Last night he had gone to bed early, but not without having seen much to unsettle him; and now this Empire-building Scotsman with the informative manner was more than he could cope with.

'Excuse me, I must get on with my – that is – I – you, will you excuse me?'

And he hurried out of the room.

At half past twelve, Mavis Woolston, the third house-maid, went up from the kitchen where Mr Ferrier the chauffeur had been showing her a novel called *O Mattress Mine* which he had found on the floor of the Daimler after the treasure hunt in Saffron Walden, to the bedroom occupied by Mrs Magda Crawshay. There was no need to knock. Bedrooms were never locked in Dymmock, and once she had found a Mr Spencer strapping a Mrs Enge to the bedpost. Mr Spencer had not been angry at the interruption. Mrs Enge was not awake. Perhaps Mrs Crawshay would be in an interesting position. Mavis entered the room anxiously. Mrs Crawshay was not in sight, but her umbrella was open on the bed.

Christopher Garvin was sure that he felt more curious than anyone in the house. Nobody's head had ever been so hot and so full of holes. He had drunk last night because it was the thing to do. The party had grown really terrible; Mrs Crawshay had removed her dress to show her boxer's bite; Gordon, before falling to sleep, with his head on an ottoman covered, for reasons that Hilary never explained, with paper doilies, had sung out of tune, thumped the piano keys with his elbow, and told Albert Ponting that he loved his smile; Captain St John exhibited his locket and the three curly hairs he said he had found in a hangman's bath; the cat could do four tricks, all vile, and Hilary Byrd had taken the party into his 'little den', but Christopher would not think of that.

He sat down at his bedroom table, refusing to notice what it was made of, and wrote a letter to Eric Wetley:

Dear Silly,

I'm feeling so absolutely awful you mustn't swear if you can't make head or tail of this higgledy piggledy letter. You mustn't be cross, I can't stand it this morning. The rain's falling like a shroud, *just* like a shroud. I can't write a thing. I tried to do a poem on the first night at Dymmock, but the words wouldn't come. I think I'd stagnate in Suffolk. I told Hilary that I thought I'd stagnate in Suffolk, and he agreed. I wish we could play Purcell together. Nobody likes music here. There is a gramophone, but the horn's full of postcards. Women. Hilary's awfully Lower Fourth. Did I tell you Wishart's are going to do my *Whining Schoolboy*. You know: Jaques. *As You Like It* or something. Seven and a half on the first five hundred. Magda Crawshay's here, though I can't think why she was invited. A man called Gill got sick exactly at midnight. Not the sculptor.

There's a man called St John who's a tiny bit interesting, and of course there would be Ponting. He's everywhere. Bobbie Cameron's got the bedroom next to mine, but don't be jealous because all he thinks about is Horlick's. And squash. He's got a bag full of clubs and bats. I couldn't resist having a peep. But he's not serious, really. I think his poems are phoney. Remember me to Miles, and Rafe and Arnold. There's nothing for me to say to you: you know it all. And it still is. You know who I am. I'm
Christopher.

He went downstairs, not thinking of Eric. Captain St John stood at the foot of the stairs.
'Oh, it's you.'
'Who else could it be?'
'Hilary's not back yet.'
'I didn't know he was away.'
'Let's do something before lunch, shall us?'
'I haven't got any initiative.'
They walked together to the billiards room, laughing affectionately at the family portraits on the corridor walls, and played a hundred up and ripped the cloth.

In Captain Mervyn St John's bedroom, Rosemary Coates, housemaid, searched, with experienced deftness, the pockets of a sports coat hanging at the end of the bed. In the inside pocket were four pound notes and a photograph of a man on sentry duty, a bill from a tobacconist's, a driving licence endorsed three times, a letter from his old nurse thanking him for a present, unspecified, an envelope with Flax 34092 scribbled on it, a membership card for the Stingo Club, and a small diary. The first entry was: 'Fitz at the Crackers, seven sharp. Remember the pony. Keep mouth shut about Donald and the soap.' The last entry read: 'Beatrice not my cup of. Forget scene about the signature. No aces in Tich's again. Avoid the Up & Down, the

Bootiful, the King of Prussia, Ward's, Mrs Slesser, J.B., Bunny. Squeeze invitation from Hilary Byrd. A.1 tip from X: – something under the Haydon. Disguise: queer. I love Muriel Luther. (?) Kiss kiss kissum. Tallboy for the 3:30. "I'll never say that I was false of heart." Very quote.'

The rest of the entries were nearly all commands to himself to forget or remember. There was one indecent poem. Rosemary read it several times, glancing over her shoulder after each verse. The things people thought of.

In the right-hand flap pockets was a Sotheby's catalogue, a score card for the Middlesex *v.* Surrey match inscribed with careful drawings of pinmen playing with pinwomen, one bootlace, a *Racing Calendar*, an invitation to dinner from a socialist peer, and a large penknife. In the left-hand pocket was one sheet of paper folded in half and addressed 'To Paul Pry'. Rosemary opened the paper out and read:

Who dips his hand into this coat
Will have a dagger thro' the throat.

She folded the paper carefully again, put it back in the pocket, made the bed, hardly daring to touch the sheets that had lain so recently against the body of the mad Captain, and went down the stairs. Her hands were shaking. She had not taken anything at all. She did not want a dagger through the throat. Curiosity killed the cat. She wasn't a cat. She was Rosemary Edna Coates, housemaid, 21. As she passed the billiard-room she heard the Captain say from within: 'Now we've ripped it all up,' and the voice of another man reply: 'What a lovely green scar.'

She ran down the corridor to the servants' quarters, with Landru and Neil Cream bouncing behind her like men running on springboards. In the kitchen Mrs Evans, the cook, gave a cup of black coffee to Albert Ponting.

'Make yourself comfortable, dear,' she said. 'You're

green as a gooseberry. This'll do you all the good. It's special. Whenever you want anything you just come to me. There, that's right, drink it down. Any better?'

'Could I have a bit of bread-and-jam?' Ponting asked. 'I couldn't keep my breakfast.'

Mrs Evans hurried to the larder. Rosemary Coates stood at the door and looked at Albert Ponting. He was tall and thin and distinguished and young. She knew he was as timid as she was. They looked at each other without speaking, across the cool kitchen, both of them, for the moment, safe from the Dymmock guests.

Sipping his fourth whisky, Gordon, alone in the library, wondered who that fellow was. He may have been an authority on Burmese archaeology. He said he was in the BM. He was probably a professor. He was certainly sneering behind his spectacles. I saw him. You can't fool me. You can always fool me. Don't say that. I've put my foot in it again. He thinks I'm eccentric. I should have worn my Balliol tie. He fingered the pastelled birds. 'Silly little birds,' he said guiltily. It was his favourite tie. Who was that smug professor of archaeology to rush out of the room in the middle of a sentence? Not everybody knows about Burma. Nobody wants to know about Burma. Burma's no good. Full of teak. Bloody Burma. And a Balliol tie was a class medal. Gordon knew which side he was on. He stood on the side of the angels, but he did not relish the day when they would fly. That Burmese teakman would hang on a lamp-post high as. He took another drink and closed his eyes. It was tumbling and black and fiery in there: Ixion, Charon, Atlas and Icarus, his mother and the archaeological stranger, appeared, performed and vanished there, all at the same time, whizzing on a catherine wheel, rowing down the sewers of Paris wide as the Thames, bearing the earth and a book of maps on a turning head, dizzily floating to the sun, scolding, reproving and washing up great plates, dancing through jungles and museum like an erudite witch-doctor.

He opened his eyes. Christopher Garvin and Captain St John were looking at the bookcase. This would never do. Half past twelve on a June morning and his head was spinning. 'Heard the news?' he asked, in a cautious voice. 'Burma's fallen.'

He was sure that Christopher, at least, knew nothing at all about the East. And this Captain fellow: he looked simple enough. Gordon inspected him warily. Was that powder at his temples? There was rouge on his cheeks, professionally smoothed into the hollows.

'A French chap I know at the BM,' he began, full of confidence. Christopher and the Captain were only two of those. 'Then Bulgaria seizes Syria.' He pointed his glass at the Captain. He put the glasses on the side table in the positions of protagonists. He moved them about. 'Now the feeling in Algiers, so I'm . . .'

Christopher and Captain St John, the first, tentative intimacy of their friendship interrupted, stood, with glasses in their hands, and watched a flushed, harassed, garrulous, erratic poet wearing a funny tie assume what he imagined to be the manner and voice of a business man in the know.

By this time Mrs Evans, Rosemary and Ponting were all sitting down at the kitchen table, jam and sweet biscuits before them.

'This isn't really elevenses,' Mrs Evans said, 'because it's a quarter past one. Mr Byrd's late.'

Ponting did not wish to offend the servant nor to show himself an unconventional guest. For all his air of aloofness, he was nervously aware of his social inexperience. One shouldn't like sweets and jam; one should feel as much at home in the front of the house as in the kitchen. But one didn't.

'What sort of a man is Mr Byrd? I mean, is there always a party on here?'

He looked with great earnestness at Mrs Evans. Rosemary opened her mouth to speak, but Mrs Evans said quickly, 'The Master entertains all the year round. This is Liberty Hall. He's very generous, Mr Ponting. His father was Sir and he had three wives, Miss Hooper, Lady Byrd, and Miss Eggerton.'

'All at the same time, too,' Rosemary said.

They were both proud to share in the fame and shame of everything that went on in the front of the house.

Only by keeping her eyes fixed on the young Mr Ponting's nice, strange face could she forget the note in the Captain's pocket and the laugh coming out of the billiards room.

Ponting was conscious of her interest, but did not dare return her look. The girls and women he knew were all either very remote, untouchably groomed and aware, acquaintances' wives surrounded always with the odorous mystery of the double bed, or flash and giggling, or Slade-fringed and dressed like early John models, or talking about hymens in loud voices and chasing him through crowded parrot parties even into the anonymous safety of the gentlemen's lavatory.

Rosemary was altogether different. He could not bring himself to smile, as he could readily smile without feeling when any of his London women friends or enemies were near, at the plump, curly, rosy-cheeked housemaid with the unfashionable breasts and the bright eyes, willing to be naughty at the first excuse.

He heard a car draw up outside the front door. Mrs

Evans jumped to her feet and scurried about the kitchen. 'It's Mr Byrd. Hurry up, Rosemary.'

'I'll see you again, Mrs Evans. Thank you for being so kind.' He bowed. It was a low, respectful bow, from one intelligent adult to another. He made, he imagined, rather an attractive figure. There was raspberry jam at the corner of his mouth, and he looked, bowing there, even younger than his twenty-one years.

Mrs Evans said, 'Come again, dear, when there's anything you want.'

'Goodbye, Mr Ponting,' said Rosemary.

He gave her a little smile, for the first time. They both blushed.

He walked out of the kitchen into the corridor, past the billiard-room, towards the cavernous dining hall. He heard his host's voice and the high, squeaking voices of several children.

Derek Gill was absorbed. He was very keen on his subject. Long bicycle rides when an undergraduate, in England and on the Continent, had laid the foundations of his cautious taste. Dymmock satisfied at once his feeling for the safe, and for the odd. The house was built upon a slight eminence, giving it command, rare in that flat country, of an extensive prospect. From the terrace the garden fell in graceful waves to the park down which a mile-long ride dwindled to a fantastic gatehouse. In the distance a yellow sea of corn bore up church hulls, extravagant and massive.

Derek had examined the gatehouse before breakfast. It had been built by Dominic Byrd, a friend of Beckford's. The plan had been roughed out with his thumb in claret on the cloth after dinner, and the gatehouse had been begun a few weeks later by specially imported Italian workmen.

It had not weathered well. The tiles had fallen out – it was

built in a Persian, not a Gothic style – the stucco peeled, and
the whole mass become creepered and grey-green. The sort
of thing you imagined drunken prospectors stumbling upon
in Indo-China. Summer trippers admired it very much
indeed. Artistic.

The house itself was quite another matter. Over the
Saxon manor a castle had been built at the beginning of the
twelfth century; this had been destroyed during the Wars
of the Roses and a Tudor mansion erected at right angles
to its ruin. A fire had broken out after a party given by that
Byrd who was a friend of Rochester's, leaving only a wing
remaining; and Wren had built the harmonious mass which
faced the gatehouse. Wren's gatehouse had been pulled
down by Dominic. In 1700 Dymmock formed three sides
of a square: the old castle, the unharmed Tudor wing, and
the Wren façade. Dominic Byrd had rehabilitated the
medieval side of the square in the finest neo-Gothic manner.
His son left the estate heavily over-burdened by his whim of
building a fourth side to this quadrangle – 'to keep out the
country', as he explained. He never moved outside his
library save to the courtyard resulting from the great
Regency block erected by Barry, which joined Strawberry
Hill to Wren, opposite the Tudor side.

These extravagances had crippled the Byrds. Every bit
of land had been sold by Hilary's grandfather. His father had
married well, but only well enough to keep the great house
going. By inhabiting a quarter of the house only, Hilary
managed to go on living there. It was not very comfortable.
The Wren rooms were covered and shuttered; Barry's
nobly irrelevant block was unused; the exquisite Tudor
brick was used as a backcloth only. For Hilary preferred to
live in the original ruin so oddly restored by his great-great-
grandfather.

The back of the house was now the front; the gatehouse

was closed and the gates locked. You approached Dymmock Hall by a rough, a very rough, cart-track, over which Hilary Byrd loved to hurtle in his Bugatti. If you arrived, you went in through the Beckford baronial gates into the courtyard. Sometimes you went on into the lily pond, a legacy of Hilary's American mother. Hilary sometimes put pike into it.

Gill moved from century to century in an aesthetic trance. The delicious shock of moving round the perfect Wren front to the softly patined sixteenth-century brick; to turn a corner and come upon the Castle of Otranto; to know that another turn would bring him to one of Barry's most inspired creations. It was almost too much. It *was* too much.

His eye travelled blissfully up the neo-Gothic inconsequence and was arrested by something white against the grey. He gasped, then looked again. A naked woman was doing a sort of wire walk along the parapet, balancing professionally with an open umbrella. He looked wildly round. A car was rocketing over the cart-track. No help there!

He hurried into the house.

'Help,' he cried. 'Help' in the high Gothic hall. Servants came running. 'A madman – I mean a madwoman. On the roof.'

One of the maids screamed. Doors were flung open; and a new noise was added as the powerful car roared up and stopped in a shower of gravel.

Mavis Woolston scampered up the stairs. She'd known the umbrella meant something. Such a prim young gentleman, no wonder he'd been shocked. Porson and Ferney had lumbered out with a blanket, and the other servants were all yelling 'Jump'. But not Mavis – she'd made straight for the back stairs. She burst breathlessly into the bedroom. There were two open umbrellas on the bed. Mrs Crawshay was leaning out of the window. 'Bloody fools,' Mavis heard her say as she pulled her head in and turned back into the room. Then: 'What do *you* want? Can't one get a minute's peace in this house?'

She made a fine if battered figure as she stood facing the startled maid. Mrs Crawshay had been knocked about in a good many stormy seas, but she'd kept her yachtish lines.

'I beg your pardon, madam. I thought you might need me.'

'You might get me a decent umbrella. These are both too heavy to balance with. I found them in the cloakroom last night. Cut along and try and find me a parasol, there's a good girl. Double quick. And bring me a brandy-and-soda.'

'Very good, madam.' Mavis retreated backwards out of the room. Her morning was turning out quite well after all.

The noise of a car, a woman's scream and the surprise of children's voices brought out Christopher Garvin and Captain St John from the library. They had been listening to a long and repetitive mis-explanation of the future of the East, and were glad of the interruption. Gordon, becoming more didactic as the morning wore on, had lost himself and his argument in a fury of detail and elaborate hearsay; he had shifted his armies of glasses with more and more fervent lack of enthusiasm as he caught, every now and then, the suggestion of a smile under the Captain's moustache, and a look of quickly concealed contempt or boredom in Christopher's big eyes.

Now the others were gone, he settled back in his chair. Women were being hysterical in the hall; men's voices were shouting unintelligible instructions; nothing mattered at all. He saw himself as a man of affairs tired after a busy morning with experts from the oriental department of the Foreign Office; he knew himself to be a long and awkward poet, lolling, three-quarters drunk, on a chair in someone else's library, after a morning of bewilderment and incompetence. But the knowledge did not seriously affect him. Lord Gordon, General Gordon, old G. of the F O, stretched out for the whisky bottle and the glass which had been Burma.

The turmoil of servants was almost soothing to Garvin and the Captain: Gordon had a curiously flat and rasping voice and the eye of the Ancient Mariner. They had not been able to move. Now Garvin leant against a suit of armour, watching the fighting maids. Mr Ferney, the chauffeur, was trying to separate two girls whom he called 'Mavis' and 'You'. 'You', it appeared, thought that there was a mad dog upstairs.

At this moment Hilary Byrd entered. He saw the flurry of white caps and aprons, a flash of underclothes, Mrs Evans swaying with excitement at the foot of the stairs, Christopher indolent against a mail bosom, Ponting, in a corner, trying to draw no attention, rather green in the subdued light, almost subaqueous in the shadows. The Captain had rushed for brandy, but finding no one except Christopher calm enough to drink it, he drank it himself. Derek Gill was running about from person to person, trying to explain in a thin, gnat-like voice.

Hilary Byrd, at the door, heard: 'Get apart, you.' 'Hold her, Mavis.' 'Ooo, he's got the rabies.' 'Nobody's got the rabies, it's only a lady.' 'It was only a lady without her . . .' 'Brandy-and-soda' (howled from upstairs).

'Girls!' said Hilary Byrd.

The noise stopped. The two maids and the chauffeur stood in the middle of the hall like frozen dancers, a hand motionless in mid-air that was to have muffled a mouth, a foot poised ready to hack the shins.

'May I introduce six friends?' said Hilary Byrd, smiling gently at the company. 'Six small friends.'

He brought out a large dog-whistle on a string from his monocle pocket and blew three times. There was a patter of little feet: little squeals came from outside the door; there were noises that might have meant that the new visitors were quarrelling as to who should enter first, and giving one another little slaps and pushes in the back. Then six very small men appeared, all at once, with their hats in their hands. They bowed.

'Welcome to Locksley Hall,' said Hilary returning their bow.

The tallest of the new visitors, a bald, grave, butlerish man of about three-foot-nine, with a wrinkled face and large, shining ears, and hands tiny as a mole's forepaws, sheathed in black gloves, approached the giants of the house, though not without compulsion: ten other little hands, all similarly gloved, assisted him. 'Thank you, Lord Tennyson,' he said. 'The six Mr Hartleys are honoured to be the guests of Locksley Hall.'

He turned fiercely on the Mr Hartleys in the background. They raised a discreet cheer.

The servants retired. The guests came forward to greet the midgets.

The Mr Hartleys shook hands all round, and said it was a very rainy day, especially for June. They said they hoped the weather had not spoiled the cricket.

The gong rang.

The afternoon sun streamed through the library windows and lit up the whisky bottle. Gordon twitched in his chair and woke up. The sensation was rather like being hanged. He was covered with sheets of *The Times*, and someone had removed his new buckskin shoes. He found them on the floor. A little note beneath them said 'Prairie Oysters in the dining room'.

He looked very childish as he smoothed his hair and straightened his symbolic tie.

He arrived in the hall at the same time as Mrs Crawshay. She was coming by the banisters. She was wearing a bathing suit so much worn that it looked like dirty lace.

'Hi, there,' said Gordon shakily.

'Hoorah,' she cried and 'Damn' as her descent was painfully and gothically ended.

She took his arm and they moved towards the dining room. There was an awful noise. They opened the door and went in.

'Speech! Speech!' cried five faces, barely visible above the dining table. And a sixth face on tiny shoulders heaved up, and a tiny pair of legs balanced a two-foot body on the Adam chair. His dimpled fists on the board, Mr Hartley addressed them, but not very much could be heard in the confusion. 'Auspicious occasion' and 'very great honour' struggled with 'pass the brandy' and 'pop him in the wine cooler'.

Then Hilary Byrd saw Mrs Crawshay and led her forward. Gordon followed sheepishly.

'What *is* all this?' said Mrs Crawshay.

'A celebration, my dear Magda. I have been greatly honoured. Gordon, congratulate me. Don't you think I shall make a charming Poet Laureate?'

'Congratulations,' said Gordon. He wished he were feeling more alert. He was out of his depth.

'Yes. I only opened the letter during luncheon.'

'But . . .'

'No, don't say it. Spare my blushes.'

'I mean . . .'

'They read his book of parodies by mistake.' Christopher Garvin was acid.

'Who?'

'The Prime Minister.'

'. . . the health of His Gracious Majesty's new Poet Laureate.'

Shrill cheers and hearty little claps came from the luncheon party.

'Ow! He's bitten my ankle.'

One of the midgets was having games under the table.

'Let go, you little beast.'

'Put 'em in the pond.'

The midgets, bawling indignantly, were hustled from the room.

'You're pulling my leg,' said Gordon. His head was still spinning.

'Not the least bit in the world,' said Hilary, and handed him a letter.

Its authenticity was beyond question.

'Well, my dear, this is all fairly funny, isn't it?'

'Do you think it's a practical joke?'

Christopher Garvin hated practical jokes. His tortured adolescence had been one long jump from booby-trap into apple-pie bed.

St John finished drying his hands, and they left the bathroom.

'No, actually, I don't. Let's go to Bluebeard's room.'

Christopher shuddered.

'All right.'

It was up two flights of stairs in an octagonal tower.

'The door's locked.' Christopher sounded relieved.

'Doesn't matter.' St John took a pipe-cleaner out of his pocket, twisted it, and bent over the lock. The door opened with a click.

'You *are* clever.'

It was a gloomy little room, where Monk Lewis might

39

have written. Perhaps he had. 'Hilary wouldn't let me stay last night, and I wasn't sorry.'

'I find it rather amusing. Look at that, for instance.'

It was a picture of a pretty girl. Her hair was theatrically peroxided, and the smirking face lay coyly against her two clasped hands. She was wearing a sequined dress, cut low in a Paris 1880 style. The dress ended just below the waist, and so did she. Her legs had been amputated high up the thigh. 'To my darling Hilary,' ran the violet-inked inscription, 'from Lorna.'

Christopher shuddered. 'I think it's *horrid*.'

St John didn't answer. He was looking at a picture of a fat woman, beside her an elegant Hilary standing in evening cloak, his top hat rakish. Underneath was written 'Brussels 1930' in a neat Greek script.

They found a coil of hangman's rope; a set of illustrations to the *120 Jours de Sodome* by a young German; a number of 'curious' little Japanese objects; a series of framed pathetic letters beginning 'Hilary my dearest'. The last letter in the series was written on lined notepaper in an illiterate hand. It said what the girl's father would like to do to Hilary, and that his only daughter had died 'telling me not to do nothing to hurt you'.

Hilary's precise comment on this one was '£50'.

There were pictures of several tattooed ladies, and a whole row of photographs of the same bearded lady. These were of quite recent date.

'Old-fashioned idea of vice, hasn't he? Just an ordinarily dirty little mind, I suppose, really.'

'I think it's all perfectly disgusssting.'

Christopher was looking, tear-dimmed, at a charming nude diving boy grinning from ear to ear. 'Tahiti '29' indexed that one.

A clamour rose from below.

'Come and help at once! Quickly!'

They were the shrill shocked tones of Derek Gill.

'That little man's always on the spot, isn't he.'

They craned out of the window down into the courtyard.

'Mr Hartley's been dragged under by a shark.'

'My God,' they heard Hilary's voice. 'It must be my beautiful pike.'

There was a lot of shouting and splashing. Christopher suddenly drew back into the room. He began to cry, hysterically.

St John patted him on the shoulder. 'Never mind. Just think of it as an addition to Hilary's museum.'

'I want to go home,' sobbed Christopher. 'I want to go home.'

CHAPTER THREE

CATS' FUGUE

'Yes. I was staying there when he got the news.'

'Dirty little beast. I'd like to wring his neck.'

'Why don't you?'

'I've half a mind to. God, I could tell you things about him even Tom Driberg wouldn't print.'

'You'd be a public benefactor.'

'I've always wanted to commit the perfect murder. Byrd's the perfect victim all right.'

'Have another drink, Bob.'

'Thanks. I mean, I tried to fit in there – a fellow ought to be all things to all men. But that midget business stuck in my gullet.'

'Who else was there?'

'Oh, Magda Crawshay; and that wet, Ponting; and a fellow called St John; and Christopher Garvin; and another chap – Gill, I think his name was – who said he was on *Hill and Dale* and talked about Burma all the time.'

The tweedy figures downed their drinks and left the bar. It always pleased Gordon to be able to talk 'naturally' with another member of the advertising firm he worked for.

At 3.30 p.m. Basil Minto rang up William Dudley.

'Hullo, Bill. Sorry to get you out of bed.'

'It's all right. I was dressing.'

'I know you won't have seen the newspaper so you don't know who's the new Poet Laureate, do you?'

'No. Do you? *Go away, Mrs Porter.*'

'Guess who?'

'I don't know. Day Lewis?'

'Hilary Byrd.'

'Strange.'

'My dear, it's menacing. I mean, the one cultural appointment. The one chance for this Fascist government to *do* something. Show their belief in what we're fighting for by choosing a sound man, a man like Jack Atkins. It's really too infernally naughty. I can't tell you how I feel. I mean, it's not the actual appointment that matters, it's the symbol. Old Crewe only read one poem of his and gave him the Canary straight away. Yes, that's really true, I heard it from a man who knows his secretary. He was indecently drunk, too.'

'Well, I shouldn't believe what he says then. Leave the tortoise alone, Mrs Porter. *He's not dead. He's thinking.*'

'No, old Crewe. The night they blew up the gardener. It was a *parody* of Day Lewis. Everyone knows what a wart Byrd is. Frightful queerie, my dear. Slept with a horse in his last term: I heard that as an absolute fact. What did you say? From the horse? No, really, I mean it's humiliating. He'll be given every opportunity to sneer and jibe at every decent thing left in the country. He'll do odes on naval victories and things, and make them stink. They shouldn't allow it. I've a good mind . . .'

'What are you going to do? Murder him? *Mrs Porter, please go away. I know there are nettles in my room. Your brushing and mopping when I'm trying to talk won't help.*'

'No, no, not murder him. That would be too much of a compliment. I'm going to expose the whole business in my Postscript in the next number of *Sunrise.*'

'And when I did my exercises the whole bloody house went hysterical. I asked for a brandy-and-soda – one, love – and the bloody little skivvy said I was a mad dog. Two,

43

love. The oddest house I've ever been in in my life. Three, love. There, you've knocked the ball into the curry again. Never mind, wipe it. Wipe it! There's a chemise on the bed.'

Albert Ponting, playing ping-pong with Magda Crawshay in her bedroom, picked up a piece of dark cloth and wiped the ball. Very soon he was going to be ill. He felt the old, green nausea rise up in him like a trout through weeds. It must be the heat. He served. Mrs Crawshay drove the ball back straight at his face.

'You mustn't be so nervous,' she said as he cowered against the wall, 'you've got a beautiful soul. You remind me of Bramwell Booth. There's an affinity somewhere. Oh, and then the pike bit Mr Hartley and Hilary made him take ether and Captain St John and Hilary took him all round the house, up and down the stairs, in a pram. A pity you missed that. You spent too much time in the kitchen.'

'It isn't right,' Ponting said, trying not to look, through his one good eye, at the sight of Mrs Crawshay scratching her back against the bedrail. She was dressed in a home-made patchwork overcoat and nothing else. 'It isn't right that a man like that should be made Poet Laureate. He isn't a bit creative and he's the nastiest man in the world. It's all right in surrealism, but it's horrible to make a midget eat what they made him eat after dinner. It's a wonder they didn't make them all ill for days.'

'They did. Ha, they put him up the chimney. I like a bit of fun. I like a bit of fun,' she shouted suddenly and hit herself so hard on the chest that she tottered, spluttering, about the room, from the washstand with the washbowl full of fur and newspapers to the escritoire with the half-eaten breakfast on it.

'There are lots of poets who really could do the job well. I know lots, young and really creative and original, even if they do only come from the suburbs. Hilary Byrd shouldn't be allowed. He's beastly. He hasn't got any taste and he hates *everything*. I'd like to see someone beat him to death.'

Mrs Crawshay's coughing had abated. She opened her patchwork overcoat to show him her muscles. He kept his eyes fixed firmly on the furthest wall. 'I could break his arms and throw them out of the window,' she boasted. She pulled her coat round her again. 'I will,' she said.

In the morning room of the Peripatetic Club, Sir Frank Knight put away his fifth large whisky-and-soda. The young member who was paying felt well rewarded. This was the sort of thing he'd missed at Cambridge – rich ripe talk about men and books; reminiscences of the worthies whom Sir Frank had known when he was young and had just commenced lickspittle. He seemed to have known them all. Great talk of wine with Saintsbury (Knight drank practically nothing but whisky, but loved to babble of vintages); days in the saddle with Blunt (Knight was a very bad horseman, but gentlemen had to do it); long nights with Lord Haldane ('He told me, long after the others had gone up to bed, the true story of his life. I am bound in honour not to repeat it. Macmillan went down on his knees to me, but I had given my word'); talk of life and letters with Hardy (all of whose later poems he had written); and, now, the scandal of the new Poet Laureateship.

'Crewe offered it to me, but I refused. The knighthood I was compelled to accept, but this was different. But I never for one moment imagined that this would happen. Only thirty-three! I'd do something about it, but it might be misconstrued. Austin Byrd was a member here, and my wife knew Lady Byrd well, but I know very iittle about the boy and what little I know I don't like. I once offered to go down to address some society he was president of at

Eton and he replied on a picture postcard!' (Hilary had written, 'We don't like Old Etonians here.') 'Then, all this flying business: I heard from my brother-in-law, who knows a fellow in the Treasury whose son's a friend of young Byrd's, that the whole thing was a mistake. He was very drunk' (Sir Frank looked extremely disapproving. His glass was empty) 'and was really trying to commit suicide. The landing in New York was all an accident. And his poetry! He's only written two books – one was banned and the other's principally parodies. Would you mind pressing the bell?'

Three women, in Sadie Lowenstein's expensive drawing room hung with fashionable, arid paintings chosen or painted by her friends and confidential enemies, discussed the unpopular appointment all through the afternoon. The teacups, which did not contain tea, were rattled angrily; the cake from Gunter's was cut, by each in turn, as though it were a reputation; with pale, ringed hands they stroked backwards the fur of the Siamese cats upon their laps as though it were a dead lover's hair. That lover would have died unmentionably, drowned in a hot bedroom on a viscid night, in the middle of another 'scene', a twisted mouth kissing and reviling her as she gladly gave up the impossible relationship founded on suspicion, mischief, treachery, and nymphomania. Prudence Whittier and Mona Boylan had broken up one more marriage the week before last, broken it 'for *her* sake' as they always said, and were still glowing with goodwill. Sadie Lowenstein had found a man with a glorious figure; he was the true lover of a dear friend who had once been seduced by Sadie's first husband. Three happy, intelligent, tiddly women, with the faces of the damned, chattered about the Laureateship. Sometimes the mascara ran. This was the best scandal since the young

46

woman who was in love with Mona Boylan had 'married' Prudence out of spite, and borne a baby whose parentage she would not explain, and left the baby in chinchillas on Sadie's very well-sprung couch. One by one they laid their plans for the destruction of Hilary Byrd by complicated malice. And when the butler showed out Prudence and Mona into the sun, they wore the traumatic expressions of undiscovered poisoners.

'He'd've beat him easy if he hadn't run into that right hook.'

'All very well, but he *did* run into it, didn't he? He had Jack's left in his nose all through the fight like he thought it grew there.'

'He took 'em all when he was going back.'

'Certainly he did. He was going back all through the fight. If you *call* it a fight.'

'Bet you he beats him in the return.'

'He'll never get a return. He's finished.'

'What's Bill Evans say in the *Star*?'

'Never mind what Evans says. Have a drink.'

'A nice Bass. Here's the *Star*. I say, Charlie, take a look at this feller. The new Poet Laureate, it says. He's the spit'n image of that feller we saw in Brussels the time Curly got beat by the wop.'

'It *is* the same feller.'

'Don't be silly. It can't be. Poet Laureate! The funniest bloody Poet Laureate *he'd* have made. Do you remember that nigger with the razor chasing him all round the place?'

'Cor, yes. And the fat woman going after them screaming her tits off.'

'Poet Laureate!'

'I don't think. What's yours?'

47

'Isn't he lovely? You could tell he was a poet.'

'Gentleman, too. Oxford and Cambridge.'

'Don't be so soft. Poets don't wear beards any more.'

'They're romantic though.'

'Bet that one could be romantic. Without a beard. What's the good of a beard?'

'Mabel, you are rawful!'

'Where's the paper say he lives?'

'Dymmock Hall. He inherited it. His picturesque Suffolk seat.'

'Pity there isn't a picture of his picturesque seat.'

'Mabel, you are rawful!'

'He's much better looking than Robert Taylor.'

'Wouldn't it be lovely to know him. Drive down to Suffolk. Hundreds of servants. A large park, with deer and things. Anna Neagle coming to tea. The moon on the old stained glass.'

'Don't be so soft.'

'Ring the bell. We're nearly there.'

'Look there's Charlie and Bert waiting.'

'Sitting on their picturesque seats.'

'Mabel, you . . .'

'What do you think of the new Poet Laureate, Mr Jones?' The poet at the Roebuck counter leant forward with his mouth open for information, his eyes glazed by an hour's rapid drinking with the great painter.

There had been no conversation.

Hercules Jones put his glass down. He raised his head. He set back his magnificent shoulder. There was a rumble as of an anchor being heaved from the ocean bed. His voice was rusty, and startlingly loud, as if he had not spoken for a year.

'I knew his father before you were born,' he said.

48

It was the only criticism of the Poet Laureate he was, from that day on, ever known to express.

Slender as the deer in their park the two sisters were walking. Their noses quivered elegantly; their long bony fingers curled back like corn. Their elegant gowns of antique design gathered the dew on the lawn under the window. Their brother was playing Liszt in the music room.

'Such things should not be permitted, Lucretia.'

'Taste is dead, my dear Crystal.'

'Better that he were dead with it.'

'It's not good to think of such things.'

'One must face the things they call facts.'

'Perhaps, Crystal, it is a duty.'

'Hush, Lucretia, now Philip is playing Scarlatti.'

'It *is* somebody's duty.'

Calm as Borgias and as lovely they glided into the great house.

The long bar at Henekey's in High Holborn was crowded. From one of the den-like booths they looked out on the English.

'Not one of them with the guts of a rabbit,' said Mac-Manus.

'Empire-builders!' O'Brien laughed bitterly into his whiskey.

'An Empire of bloody rabbits,' rasped Sidney Gorman, who came from Australia.

'A most interesting phenomenon not unworthy of a philosopher's contemplation,' pronounced Bert Ostler, who came from Lancashire, but whose art was a gulf between himself and his fellow countrymen.

'Ah well, it won't last much longer,' said Mahaffy, with a sort of secretive cheeriness.

'You're right,' agreed foxy young Mallow, a cockney to the core, but saved by a grandfather from County Sligo.

Drinks were ordered all round, two Scotch, two Irish, a Guinness, and a ginger beer for Ostler. They were strict at the clinic.

'Well, they've got themselves a proper bloody Poet Laureate, anyhow.' Gorman was getting fighting drunk.

'Old one was pitiable. Contemptible and pitiable. Good Christ.'

'I'm not sure that I agree with you, O'Brien. I'm his executor, you know, and a lot of the unpublished stuff is remarkable, really.'

'No doubt,' said MacManus, 'remarkable drivel.'

'No, really. And there are some letters from Dowson and Middleton; and a hotel bill of Wilde's; and part of a diary of Johnson's; and the whole of the Beardsley–Smithers correspondence.'

'Better make yourself *this* man's executor. There'll be some pretty remarkable posthumous dirt there.' Mahaffy smiled, twisted, knowing.

'He's young; and vital enough to last most of us out, I'm thinking.'

'I happen to disagree. There are plenty of people who'd like to put him away.'

'I'll put him away my bloody self,' screamed Gorman, who had been sulking.

'I doubt if we shall need your help, Sidney.'

'The whole filthy structure of this rotten society will be crashing in a very few months,' MacManus glowered.

'Let me get at him,' said Gorman, falling among the glasses. They carried him out, Mallow leading. He was the practical one.

The *Admiral Nelson*, a decrepit rowing boat nearly half full of water, bobbed on the choppy sea, a mile or two off the Cardigan coast. Two young men in high sea boots, corduroy trousers, and open cricket shirts sat contentedly on either side of the boat, and fished for flats. A small keg of Irish whiskey floated on the water in the boat; and every few minutes, and sometimes more often, one of the two fishermen would bend down, silently, and lift the keg up. This regular motion shook the *Admiral Nelson* like a great wave.

The two fishermen clung on to the keg for their lives.

'My turn for the big swig,' said Tom Agard. Because it was highly dangerous to drink from a barrel while standing knee-deep in water in a pitching boat that might at any moment turn right over or go straight down like a stone, it had been arranged that they should take it in turns to have a long drink and that the man whose turn it was for a quick gulp should hold the barrel.

Tom Agard drank deep. The whisky went glugging down into his whalelike belly. Little Owen Tudor held the big barrel against his chest. Tom Agard was kneeling in the water. A wave came over the side, and Owen thought of death.

'My gulp now,' he said. Agard's ponderous rising was the most dangerous moment of all. Oh, oh, Jesu. She's tossing like a horse. We're done for this time. Over we go. Great green death. Sharks and waterdogs. Old men of the sea. Davy Jones, Davy Jones, catch me, I'm coming. The staggering exchanging of the barrel, the little swallow, the dignified whisky lurch, then again the barrel dropped like a thunderbolt into water.

'It is, in some ways, a remarkably encouraging appointment,' Tom Agard said, leaning back at his ease and addressing the whole attentive sea. 'To appoint a man whose work is a studied insult to all academic balderdash: it's a charming conceit.'

He belched comfortably. He weighed between nineteen and twenty stone and had a reddish beard. He looked jovial and Falstaffian, and could be so on occasion; but his mind was more precise than Rabelaisian. Owen Tudor had a thin precise look, dark and subtle, more like a French than an English poet, and more critic than poet, at that. This, too, was misleading. Strangers would find themselves involved in Elizabethan situations, which usually ended very uncomfortably for them and very amusingly for Owen. You would start the day drinking enormously with Tom, and find yourself at the end of it listening to a lucid criticism of the works of Webern; whereas a day with Owen beginning with an analysis of Unamuno would very likely end in the bear pit at Whipsnade or in an aeroplane flying to an unknown destination. Obviously enough, when they were together, like the Chinese metaphysicians, they 'combined their information', as it were, and felt in harmony.

'Where is that ham, you gross buffoon?'

'My dear little friend, you are sitting on it. Get up and we will eat.'

When they had bailed out the results of this manoeuvre, Owen continued, his face full of ham and pickles.

'A charming conceit – oh yes. I'm not complaining about the appointment.'

'No, indeed, but it's a pretty puzzle. I was up with Byrd. I remember throwing him into the Trinity fountain. He bore no malice; and I made settings for those early parodies of his. You remember the music was parody, too. The Ravel one was rather good as I remember. But not a nice man.'

'You're a puritan. Mine for the big swig.'

The proof pages of Owen's new poems were severely damaged.

'Never mind. Give the printer something to think about.'

'Why does one never catch anything? It's pleasant here but why don't we sit at home?'

He looked fatly at the tall Georgian house barely visible across the bay.

'We seem to be a long way from things. Let's row back. I'll steer.'

'You will not, you triple-bellied drunkard.'

'Very well. Very well. Where are the oars?'

There were no oars. Owen began to speak.

'Tut tut!' said Tom. 'You waste breath. It's an omen. We shall catch something. And we can continue our discussion in peace. Mine for the big swig.'

Oliver Fry was making a surrealist object in his neat, clinical studio. On the polished work table lay a Victorian corset, a moose's head imported, at considerable cost, from North America, several abominations, a pair of spiked steel garters, dogs' teeth plaited on a string and a woollen banjo. They were to be elements in Oliver's new creation: 'Imprisonment of a Nail'.

It was past midnight. 'When evil and disorder are not abroad, no artist should lift the somnambulist mountain of his brush,' Breton had said, translated by Paul Gravey. Oliver, who always felt dull and sleepy by half past eleven, could not forget these apocalyptic words. Well fed, unemotional, wanting to go straight to bed where he knew he would dream about dividends and decent young women well brought up, who kissed him on the forehead and told him not to bother any more, he sighed, compressed his lips, and began again the bewildering task of erecting an obscene monument to disorder out of his clean, unhappy mind.

His face was thin, pale, scrupulous, polite, lined by the anxieties that resulted from burning the candle at both ends literally, wrecking a sound digestion to procure bad dreams, being pestered for money by other dreamers, and having to beat and manacle the young women he would wish to cuddle. He did not mind doing his duty. He was conscientious and amenable to any discipline. He did not deny that each man must carry a cross; but sometimes he wondered why he had allowed his own to be made of mouse-fur and boiled wire.

He was sticking nails through the corset, in the usual way, when the door-knocker rang. It was that kind of a door-knocker, and Oliver had had a lot of trouble in designing it and then in getting the electrician to wire it for him. He still remembered how the electrician had said: 'You want the knocker to ring, sir? I can arrange to 'ave water pipes where the bloody bulbs are, if you'll excuse me, sir. Pull the switch and drown your bloody self. No offence.'

'All very good ideas,' Oliver had remarked. 'Get on with the knocker, my man.'

Oliver opened the front door. Albert Ponting stood outside in the rain. He was phosphorescent. Oliver invited him in, and, in the light of the hall, saw that the phosphorescence was fortunately a trick of the eyes. Half-way up the stairs, Oliver rejected the material explanation. He had, at least, been given a vision of the night; a slight one, it was true, and over very quickly, but none the less sinister or miraculous. Ponting, he noticed, was still glowing from under the skin. Oliver had seen a tree in a garbage field, shining with dead mackerel. Albert Ponting, the Walton Rimbaud, might have hung on that tree and lit up the night.

In the studio Ponting criticized the first stages of the 'Imprisonment of a Nail'. 'Is that *quite* ghastly enough, do you think?' pointing to the necklace of dog's teeth round the corseted moose. 'Now, that *is* terrifying, Oliver. That's frankly bestial. A dream in steel,' touching the spiked garters with a caressing abhorrence not altogether affected.

'There's a room in Hilary's house – I was down at Dymmock for the weekend, you know – you simply must see, Oliver. A woman without any legs and . . .'

'Isn't that rather trivial?' Oliver asked. He did not want to hear what else was in that room. He supposed he would have to see it now, but that was a duty to come. An invitation to 'A Laureate-Warming Party' had arrived in the morning. He could not refuse. All the young and old horrors, photographers and gossips, whom he financially supported, would be there in their squabbling dozens.

'He was rude as anything about the movement,' Ponting said. 'He told me that Shirley Temple frightened him more than Max Ernst did, and he said John Collier was a better draughtsman than Magritte.'

'But he was a foundation member!' Oliver said in alarm. 'He attended all the meetings at Lyons' Corner House.' This was treason and worse: this was the sense that he had always himself concealed so well. He felt like a Jesuit detecting heresy.

Ponting viewed his friend's set, strained expression with alarm. He didn't want his evening expedition to come to nothing. 'By the bye, Oliver, that money I spoke to you about on the telephone . . .'

He was getting desperate. This was no joke.

Surrealism was all very well – a man had to live; but this ritual murder stuff wasn't so good. Oliver looked like Assassin.

'It is a duty. Destroy the heretic and an absurd symbol of tyranny at the same time.'

Desperately, Ponting tried once more:

'Yes. But do it symbolically. Create a murder-shape, a totemic death object. You're the man to do it. The only man. And you're the only man, incidentally, I know who can get me out of this mess I'm in. . . .'

But for once Oliver Fry seemed not to hear.

CHAPTER FOUR

PARLIAMENTS OF BIRDS

It wasn't a very comfortable car. Not so bad for Tom Agard, who drove it; hellish for Owen Tudor, crushed between buttocks and gear-levers. The car went fairly fast but became white hot; and the smell of petrol was sickening. But it was a puncture that stopped them first. There was a long gravelly skid and a lurch. The car settled on one side, a sinking ship.

'Foundered.'

'Whose turn to change the wheel?'

'Don't prevaricate. Just get on with it.'

Agard extricated himself from behind the wheel with the laborious precision of a circus elephant.

Tudor sat back, moderately comfortable for the first time that day, smirking. He whistled a little tune, lit a cigarette and uncorked a bottle of Audit. Agard regarded this performance gloomily. Tudor affected to be unaware of the two great pouchy eyes. The fat man got out the jack with a lot of unnecessary noise, and fell in the dusty road with a groan. Tudor whistled a hymn tune, double time, with intervals for refreshment.

'Would you be so good as not to whistle?'

'What, not finished yet?'

'Just a drink and a cigarette. . . .'

'Not a bit of it. We're late as it is. Look lively.'

An open brewer's lorry roared by. Tudor was saved from physical violence. Agard's rage was diverted. He shouted imprecations after the lorry, his mouth filled with dust, then bent once more to his task.

*

Roger Rashleigh's enormous cigar fitted with the Duisenberg he drove, but he was out of scale with both. A very small millionaire. He drove easily and well at ninety miles an hour. Pity one couldn't drive fast in England. In Europe or America, driving Marxist friends from one conference to another, one could really move. He cornered smoothly and passed the crazy, piled-up car.

Agard had abandoned the use of the jack and was holding up the machine by the back axle, while he bawled for help. Rashleigh recognized the swollen face of the musician, and reversed. Tudor had not moved. Agard released his hold and the car relapsed once more.

'Hello, Tom,' said Roger. 'In difficulties?'

Agard advanced with a menacing buffalo's tread.

'Can I give you a lift?'

In an instant Tudor was out of the seat and scrabbling for more Audit; Agard sat down on the running board; Roger walked round his great car, invisible, and joined them.

'Going to Dymmock, I suppose? There's going to be quite a party. We can all go together.'

They got into the car.

The brewer's lorry – Halifax's Golden Prize Beer is Full of Good Cheer – which was shaking along in the direction of Dymmock Hall contained six men of letters. They sat on cases of Halifax in the open back of the lorry. Sidney Gorman, the Australian historian, had tampered with each case in turn, but had not managed to get one open. The cases were scratched, hacked, splintered. Gorman had broken two penknives and cut his thumbs.

Ostler waved his deerstalker at the broken-down car. 'Two poets,' he said. 'That seems to explain everything.'

'Tudor doesn't make sense. He drinks,' said Mallow.

'Dear God above me,' said O'Brien, 'there's only one poet

among the whole lot of you and he isn't here. He's the man who wrote *that* little poem.' He pointed to the Halifax slogan painted unsteadily on the back of the driver's cabin: Halifax's was a small dishonest concern whose products even Sidney Gorman had been heard to refer to as 'No bloody good-o', after drinking a gallon in bed.

'There isn't a breath of poetry in it at all,' MacManus shouted. He was hot and tired and covered with dust; the motion of the lorry upset his stomach; last night he had given a lecture on Burns to the empty chairs in his bed-sitting room, and bottle imps inside the cupboard had clapped and cheered. Life was catching him up again. 'It's doggerel, doggerel,' he shouted. He told them what poetry was. He gave them examples.

> '*We'll burrn the broot and fadge our coot*
> *By Whalsey's mimring whutter,*'

he recited, 'that's the real stuff.'

'What's whutter?' Gorman asked. He did not care if anyone answered him or not. His cuts were smarting. He had no idea where he was going. Without any hope of success; he struck at a case marked 'Special Golden' with Ostler's ornate walking stick.

Mahaffy said, from his corner: 'Why don't you burn the box?' He was able to make every question he asked sinister and sly. It was one of his most engaging tricks, and had lost him more friends than he had ever needed. Halifax's unbreakable case of repellent ale became, through his twinkling leer, his nods and shudders of contented malice, a symbol of English corruption, a secret meeting place of reactionary MPs, a trove of Montagu Normans. 'I've got a big box of matches,' he said. He brought them out of his pocket, slowly.

Gorman, trembling, lit a match and put it against the side

of the case. The match went out immediately. He lit another.

'No, no. Use your head, man,' said Ostler. 'Proper way is to soak box in paraffin.' He made no effort to move. It was enough to know.

'Who's got any paraffin?'

The lorry rattled on. Those are trees over there, thought Mallow. Oak trees, perhaps. That was hay; or was it corn? Which was the yellowest?

The lorry passed the barley field at a great speed.

Mallow, a nature poet with a considerable London reputation, was always bewildered by the country: the common properties of his verse grew unrecognizably alive around him. In the distance a real ploughman with a white horse moved through a field of something or other, contradicting every line of *Country Sonnets: A Sheaf* and *The Soul and the Flower* (5th thousand). The country was against him. 'Apples', that rhymed with 'dapples', were big red threats on a tree. He had never realized that the lyrical hedgerow was so tall and tangled and dark. In Theobald's Road these things took on a safe perspective. He began to long for the Angel and Crown. The bar would be crowded, celebrities falling like skittles.

The others looked uncertainly around them. There didn't seem to be any paraffin.

Rashleigh's great car rocketed past them.

'Three poets now,' said Ostler. He liked order.

'I remember,' O'Brien said, 'when I was a nipper in Sligo me old man and meself burnt down Lady Rafferty's barn. We wanted to know what she'd say. We took the door off its hinges and soaked it in petrol and the old one stole a blowlamp. In just under an hour, by Jesus, there was a fire like Hell itself and the Lady came caterwauling out. The cursing, the cursing,' he said happily. 'She hit the old fool down with her shoe, and her foot was as big as a boat, and then she had me larruped and the whole blessed afternoon cost me daddy the price of three pigs.'

'Stop the lorry,' said Mahaffy.

Ostler beat on the window. The driver pulled up. She was Mrs Burgin, the landlady of the Bells, a small, Halifax-tied house on the outskirts of London. An invaluable woman and very experienced.

'Mrs Burgin,' said Mahaffy, 'will you kindly suck out a drop of petrol from the tank for us? We want to make a little fire in the back.'

Mrs Burgin tossed her red hair. 'Suck it yourself, big boy,' she said.

The six men conferred in whispers.

'Twist her arm,' Gorman suggested. The others turned on him at once.

'Australian pig.'

'It's a dirty torturer you'd make yourself all for a bottle of muck,' said MacManus.

'We'll have to suck it in turns,' Mahaffy said. 'You begin, Mallow.'

'What shall we put it in?'

'Doesn't Mallow wear boots?' said Mahaffy.

Gorman said, 'Give her The Key.'

They made Mallow remove one boot, but could not make him give the other up. 'That's a real friend!' said Mahaffy. They called Mallow an Englishman, and climbed out of the lorry.

After several preliminary cursings and spittings, Mallow managed to catch quite a lot of petrol in his mouth. 'Hold it!' MacManus shouted. 'Don't try to say anything! Who's taken the boot?'

When they had filled the boot and had seen to Mallow, calming him with promises of the first bottle, they climbed back and poured the petrol over the Halifax case. Mrs Burgin drove on.

Soon there was a roaring little fire. The straw on the floor of the lorry caught with a blaze. Shouting and jostling, the six writers kept jumping away from the flames and encouraging each other to take off his coat and put the fire out. In this confusion they drove into Dymmock courtyard.

The courtyard was full of people running. Mrs Burgin, taking no risk of an accident, guided the lorry expertly into the pond.

Albert Ponting and Oliver Fry stood by the lily pond in the courtyard: Ponting uneasily proprietary, as one who had been there before, Fry with the self-deprecatory manner he always adopted when he wasn't remembering to be over-real. It was the manner of a rich man accustomed to the company of cleverer, poorer people.

With them, three deadly nightshades, were Mona Boylan, Sadie Lowenstein, and Prudence Whittier. Sadie had her notebook out and was 'figuring' the cost of the journey from London. Mona's flabby clown's mask had slipped sideways with the strain of being in the country. The mask might have graced the pillows of a late nineteenth-century literary deathbed. Prudence was enjoying being with queer people who were at the same time established.

'Haven't you boys got anything to say?' barked Mona. Why couldn't somebody *talk*?

'We've all got culture. Have you taken a vow of silence or something? It's like being with a couple uv Desert Fathers on an off night.'

Ponting fumbled his tie. He had been enjoying his pose of aristocratic dandy out of the world. A green blush spread over his face.

Oliver stepped in: 'How do you like the house?'

'Three pounds seventeen and sixpence and ten shillings for . . .' muttered Sadie.

'It's perfectly lovely,' said Prudence. 'Elegant.'

'Looks about as elegant as a bad dream to me,' said Mona. 'Say, when does the ghost come on? I smell blood. Don't you? She turned on Ponting. 'No, you wouldn't. You're just a fish. You belong in the pond here.'

'A fish?'

'Yeah. And Fry here's a bird. A pretty dead bird, too.'

'What about the others?'

'Oh, Sadie's a snake, and Prudence is just a nice little lady *dog*. I'm a Komodo Dragon,' she concluded.

Ponting edged away.

'Well, come *on*! Can't you say something?'

Nobody said anything. It is not easy, or even safe, to swap pleasantries with a Komodo Dragon. One or two habitués of the Deux Magots had been up to Mona's weight, but they were mostly put away now.

'And another pound for luncheon, drinks fifteen . . . no, sixteen shillings and tenpence and the car . . .'

'Say, why don't you get an adding machine, Sadie? The inside of your skull must look like Wall Street after an international incident.'

'Really vurry vurry lovely. So old.'

'Gahd! We'll all get old if we stay here waiting for these two Oscars to crack an epigram. Let's go rustle up a coupla drinks. Gahd, here comes the fire-brigade.'

Roger and Owen and Tom heard the commotion, but did not move. Nothing ever disturbed Roger except the existing social order, and Tom had been at Dymmock before. Owen was far too well entertained to move from the corner where they were sitting. He commanded a view of Hilary Byrd, Sir Frank Knight, and Cornelius, the famous

Baltic playwright. Cornelius had published nothing since gaining the Nobel Prize fifteen years before. He had not needed to, and was very glad not to, as his contempt for writing was profound. He liked girls, and sailing a boat, and vodka. He never refused to go to a party when abroad and without his boat. Vodka and girls were usually provided for him, and he never had to talk. His English was limited, and had been taught him entirely by sailors in brothels and speakeasies, a source of great embarrassment to members of the PEN Club. He liked Mr Byrd: they had had some fine parties in Sweden together the year before.

Knight was in his element, toadying away. Perhaps there would be a photographer. Meantime it was enough to be seen with the great Cornelius.

'What is your opinion of Knut Hamsun, Mr Cornelius?'

''E's a bloody shit,' said the Master, tersely. He was bored. Byrd filled up his glass.

Basil Minto had finished unpacking. His clothes were an odd mixture, fitting his protean character. Suède shoes and silk socks, dirty flannel trousers, a coat bought ready-made in France, a loose tussore shirt and an old Etonian tie. The get-up of an hermaphroditic gentleman Bohemian. A tough transatlantic touch was given by the handful of cigars in the breast pocket. He was a clever, unhappy man. He looked at himself in the glass: the hands adjusting the tie were delicate and fine-boned, the face was the face of an intellectual chimp. There was a knock on the door, and Bill Dudley stumbled blindly in.

'*Eerie* house, in queerly bad taste I should have thought.'

'It's too self-conscious. Too much life for the people in it.'

'Oddly true, I do think.'

'It suits Hilary.'

'Strange.'

64

They were walking down the gloomy corridor when they heard a shriek; and Christopher Garvin appeared at a bed-room door, looked wildly round, and galloped towards them, holding up his trousers as he ran.

'Help!' he cried. 'Help! Pat Barrington's stolen my belt.'

A buxom woman came romping out of the room Christopher had left. She was wearing a kimono and brandished a schoolboy belt in her hand.

'Don't be shy,' she shouted, 'or I'll give you a regular spanking.'

Christopher moaned with terror and fled on down the dark tunnel of the house. Dudley and Minto opened, to let the roaring, tearing old girl after her prey, and watched the two disappear round a corner.

'Queerly eerie,' said Dudley.

Minto shrugged his shoulders. 'Too vital.'

They walked downstairs.

In the hall they found several bottles of vodka and Sir Frank Knight precariously sleeping on an oak settle. They went into the library.

'The whole thing centres round the Burma Road.' There was a splash of soda siphoned into a glass.

'Yes, I suppose so.'

Derek Gill had stayed on in the house in order to finish his article. Robert Gordon had arrived for the luncheon party half an hour before, and the two had cornered one another, mutually mesmerized.

'Ah, hullo, Basil. And Bill. Do you know Derek Gill, the archaeologist?'

'I always thought Mr Gill was an architect.'

'Not a bit of it. An archaeologist. Knows all about Burma. Have some whisky.'

Cornelius had, at last, rid himself of Sir Frank Knight by

giving him a short description, in the best Bowery, of the work of de Chames Choyce guy; a subject of which he knew nothing, for he read, with contempt, only the printed notices of his own productions. Sir Frank walked off to a group of coming writers who were scratching their names on a suit of armour. Cornelius was overrated. His breath smelt of spirits. Swedes never washed. Except that actress woman, what was her name. Fine figure. Nearer the bone, sweeter the meat. Bit long in the tooth, though. In a tangle of stale phrases he reached the writers before they could run.

Cornelius was left alone with Hilary Byrd. 'Dat Knight baby,' he said, pronouncing the K, 'I take him for a ride, see.' He lit another black cigar, and inhaled deeply. Now there was no need to think. There was not even any need to talk. He puffed and blew and looked at his waistcoat. That was a pretty button. He began to play with it. Hilary slipped away. Memories of Strauss waltzes came to Cornelius. Girls with bosoms, dancing. Hot mommas.

There was no pleasure or instruction in watching just one famous man admire his waistcoat and remember; the spectacle of Sir Frank's small downfall was over; the three critics moved on.

'If we go down the drive a little way,' said Owen Tudor, 'perhaps we shall see some people lying in a hedge.'

'I should think it's almost certain,' Roger said. He would have been extremely surprised, but his little pink-lidded eyes would never have shown it. His hands fluttered in a gesture of resignation. 'Anything might happen here. I knew Byrd in the States. He was engaged to an hermaphrodite called Arthur.'

'Arthur Lucy Sisley,' said Tom Agard, as they walked along. He knew everything and everybody. 'He was neither a gentleman nor a lady.'

There was a burnt deerstalker hat lying in the middle of the drive.

'Extraordinary things you see all over the place,' Roger said.

'I think,' said Tudor, 'that when I am a rich man with my own bicycle and can have beer for breakfast I shall give up writing poetry altogether and just be absolutely disgusting. This place has given me a lot of ideas.'

'You're talking like an affected guttersnipe,' Agard said.

'Oh, I don't know.' Roger hated rows. However they began, whoever was to blame for them, they invariably finished by everyone attacking him. 'Poetry, as we know it' – he made meaningless movements with his hands in the air: someone had once told him that all 'real human beings' used their hands expressively; Roger very much wanted to be a human being because he felt that he was always just a little less than one; his shadow amazed him; to put his name to a cheque was to take part in a great private swindle – 'Poetry, as we know it,' he repeated, 'is bound to die with the smash-up.' He was too self-conscious to use the word 'revolution'. He attempted to make his inadequate, and often schoolboy, euphemisms casual and yet inevitable, the words of a guy – three months in the States had done away with the old familiar 'chap', and no one could be stilted enough to call a friend a 'man' – who could see what was coming, realized what the future implied, regarded his own destruction as a matter of course, and still, through his social conscience, desired it. 'I think Owen may be quite right, you know. Just to be, and to wait. There's nothing new to say, is there, after all, I mean?'

Owen turned on him at once. Tom shook with ridicule.

'Poetry as we know it!' said Owen. He shook his small, grubby fists at the sky. 'God, God, God, to think that we should be walking in the open air in the middle of June and

67

a marvellous party going on, talking this . . . this poppy cock.'

Roger and Tom saw, for the first time, that their friend was not strictly sober; he said 'marvellous' in the wrong way; his face was flushed. Where had the little beast got it from? Tom felt a great compassion for himself. I am nineteen stone; I have a beard; I am wearing the biggest coat in England; nobody showed me the whisky.

'Poppycock indeed,' he said. 'You dare to talk of poppycock to me. Since when did you decide to talk like a Sunday critic? This party is *not* marvellous. It isn't a party at all. It is dull and middle-class and drab.'

Upstairs in Dymmock, at that moment, a woman was chasing a man, a man was making his face up, a poet was screaming, a man was planning a crime, an anarchist was shaking petrol out of his boot; downstairs, the pathics simpered, the anonymous female pick-ups ogled old artists and peers, a man in the library, out of sight, tore the pictures out of unpleasant books and put them in his pocket, women meditated upon disease and money, a temporary waiter was found asleep by the sloe gin.

'What's *happened*, I'd like to know?' Nineteen stone quivered in the heat.

'Take the company. Pedantic cadgers. Punch-drunk Swedes. Inefficient pederasts. Old Double Dutchers. Mincers and posers and soaks. Poets.' He gave Roger and Owen a nasty look. Roger was walking in a political dream. We're moving like three Nurmis, thought Owen. They must have walked nearly half a mile.

'Distinguished hacks. Incompetent drivellers,' Tom stormed in the middle of the mild day. 'Don't you dare to tell me it's exciting. It's dull as, dull as . . .' – he paused for a great dullness – 'as dull as Ponting.' This restored his good humour a little. 'Duller than Ponting,' he said. 'It's as

68

dull as Oliver Fry.' Owen added the names of two or three personal friends.

'Now Byrd isn't a dull man by any means,' Tom said. 'But he's a menace to society.'

'Good, good,' said Owen. He liked to imagine himself as a man pitted against society, a demon of the middle class destroying the detestable fabric from within.

'He's a menace,' said Roger suddenly, 'to society and to revolution. He's just an individual romantic. If I believed in violence, I'd exterminate him myself.' He made gestures: erasing a smudge, swatting a fly, swimming, embracing: they might have meant anything at all.

'Look, look,' cried Owen. Along the cornfield from the direction of Dymmock station a very large figure could be seen moving erratically.

'It's Magda Crawshay,' Tom said.

'A woman out of her period,' said Roger. It was his worst insult. He had once spent a week in her house, locked in his room, a prisoner.

'But what's she wearing?'

'What's she got over her shoulder?'

'It's a sack.'

Mrs Crawshay came nearer. The young men could see now that what she was carrying was the body of a woman: it was Yvonne Bacon, pillar of Charlotte Street, monument of the old Dome, artist, collector of celebrities, professional introducer, 'dear Yvonne, so bloody,' asleep, or drunk, or dead, or all three together.

Inside the bar parlour of the White Swan Hercules Jones crumpled his tankard and beat with it upon the counter. He raised his voice. Only Tommy Brock, editor of *Amateur*, a middle-aged disciple, could distinguish a few words in the uproar. 'Again,' 'Same,' 'More,' shook the bar china on its racks, disturbed the Scotch cattle, and drove Alice, backing away behind the counter, into a mild fit. She should have been used to the gentlemen of Dymmock by this time; they came in crowds all through the year, mad, bad, sober, howling, on piggy-back, in barrows, very dotty and distinguished, pale, insidious, ratlike men whose pictures were always appearing in the papers, raffish, oily, unseeing, dangerous, not nice, suddenly alive before her, famous artists, some of whom paid; but she had never recovered from a morning, some time ago, when Hamish Corbie, the only customer in the bar, had related the brief history of witchcraft to her, with practical illustrations. And this loud gentleman now. She had not been at all afraid of him when when he came in, he looked an old sport and none too safe in the dark. But his 'Same again, miss', simple, familiar words, made her tremble all over. He rocked, only three feet from her, in what she could only imagine was an insane rage; he roared, and beat with the ruins of his tankard; nothing would have surprised her, not even if flames had come sprouting out of his wide and hairy nostrils.

'Mr Jones wants another bitter,' said Tommy Brock.

'They say this is going to be a very odd party. I look forward to seeing you with Cornelius, Hercules.'

Jones drained the tankard, put it down. He smiled with Jovian benignity at the girl behind the counter. Frightened little creature. He winked.

'Byrd is a very curious person altogether,' said Brock. 'Not quite a gentleman really.'

'What's that?' bellowed Jones. The alarmed girl had fled into the darkness behind the bar; the wink had quite undone her. His attention was free for his companion.

'I was saying,' piped Tommy Brock, raising his voice a whole octave, 'that it would be a very odd party.'

Jones snorted contemptuously, a sardonic smile twisting

under the ragged moustache, the stained beard jutting. 'And what would you know about odd parties, I should like to know? I've been on parties when you were in diapers, *real* parties. When MacSweeney and I went on parties in the old days they lasted for weeks. Start in Haverfordwest and end in Corsica. Absinthe, none of your pernod paps.' After another furious '*odd* party, indeed', he relapsed into a sombre reverie in which beautiful women and great men drank and made love prodigiously, and no one was less than a demigod at the very least.

Dymmock railway station was enormous. A junction had been intended at that point, and the bold baronial plans of a Very Great Architect had been passed and the building rushed through in 1872; but the junction had been found to be impracticable at that spot, after all. The red elephant of a station remained, with useless platforms stretching in every direction. The station-master had made quite a pretty garden in the deep gullies of abandoned railway tracks between the unused platforms. He was planting spring vegetables when the station's only porter called him:

'Hey, Pop.'

'Train signalled?' It was a longish walk to the functioning part of the line.

'No. Man with paint on 'is face.'

Captain St John strolled up and down the deserted station. There was no refreshment room, and the vast waiting rooms were damp and chilly even on this June morning. Conscious of being watched, he turned sharply and saw the tubby porter sink less swift than Comanche or Apache into the rose garden between platforms 7 and 8. 'Damn this make-up,' he cursed. The disguise which had gained him his entry into Dymmock Hall was a constant embarrassment to him. He had very good reasons for being where he was. The introduction had been effected with the help of one of Hilary's borderline friends. It was St John's business to know a good many such; the character he was playing had not been selected at random. But it irked him, none the less. He hoped the people in the train he had offered to meet would be as freakish as himself appeared to be. He often had these 'unprofessional moods', as he called them.

The train could be heard rattling near. Half a dozen dingy coaches pulled up at Platform 1. The porter shouted 'Station', but did not say which station it was. That misleading habit was a relic of the Second Great War, when all signposts and nameboards were taken down so that the only people who could find their way about the country were enemy parachutists who had excellent and detailed maps. A young woman looked out of a first-class carriage window.

'Is this Dymmock, please?'

'Station!' cried the porter.

She looked up and down the platform and caught sight of the Captain standing near a milk churn. She opened the carriage door and stepped on to the platform. 'This is the place,' St John heard her call back into the carriage. 'I just saw a fairy.'

St John wished, more than ever, that he had chosen to appear as an Indian crystal-gazer. A yellow-faced man with long black hair followed her out. I wish I'd made myself up to look like that, St John thought: the young woman walking towards him was tall and carelessly beautiful. He determined, nevertheless, to act up to his part. 'I'm St John,' he said, with a deprecatory giggle. 'Shall we be friends?' She looked at him once, saw the thin rouge and the tasteful powder, then turned back to help the yellow-faced visitor with his bag.

'I'm Robin Shelley,' she said over her shoulder.

Two men stepped out of the last compartment: the first very slowly and uncertainly, owing to age and habits, the second gravely as befitted his reputation. Hamish Corbie lifted out a long, black, coffin-like box. J. L. Atkins placed his luggage in a row; many hat-boxes, excellent, capacious cases, a typewriter and a cat-basket. He called the porter in a polite, level voice that admitted no nonsense or argument. He was plainly, but perfectly dressed. Hamish Corbie dragged his funereal luggage behind him down the platform. He wore a suit of yellow, check plus fours, green woollen socks, and sandals.

St John was relieved to see such a visitor. If only the others had been all queer, too. But then he would not have seen the beautiful Miss Shelley; her presence was worth any humiliation. 'Oh, do come on, the party's going to be divine,' he said. He minced on to the waiting car.

Behind him, the visitors introduced themselves.

'My name is Atkins.' An impersonal bow.

'I'm Robin Shelley.'

'Ah, Mr Atkins, please do not say you have forgotten my name. That would be too much for such a great admirer of *East Slag*. I am Gold, Sigismund Gold.' The yellow-faced man rubbed his hands together, as if to make them sufficiently damp before the conventional clasp.

'Corbie,' said Hamish Corbie. He held up three long, stained fingers in the air and tapped the back of them three times with the jewelled index finger of his other hand.

They reached the car. 'Beauty shall step in first,' said Sigismund Gold, holding the door for Robin Shelley. 'Loveliness before . . .' he picked the right word delicately, 'mere makers of lovely things.' He sat very close to her.

St John drove slowly past the White Swan in the village square. He was hoping that someone would suggest a short rest and a quick drink: he needed them both. No one said a word. From the White Swan came a stamping and shouting, a banging of doors, the squeals of a young woman. 'Come here, my little beauty.' 'Let me go, let me go.' 'Easy on there, sir.' 'Come here, my little Pollyanna. Nobody's going to bite you.' The last sentence was bawled so fiercely that Captain St John accelerated at once. Thank God those oafs weren't coming to the party. It would be bad enough without them.

'Oh, what frightful, rough people,' he giggled. Nothing could help him now. Committed to a ludicrous femininity, he gossiped in a shrill voice all the way to Dymmock.

A very old carriage, drawn by a fine pair of bays, approached the gatehouse. Two tall ladies and a tiny but exquisite man sat inside. They were all three dressed with severe formality, but not in the current fashion. The carriage stopped. 'The gate's closed, my lord.'

'Then drive round, Quince. There must be another one.'

'Were you never here before, Philip?'

'No, Lucretia.'

'I am not quite sure why we are come today.'

'We have come *to see for ourselves*, Crystal.'

Little Lord Lacey pressed his pomander to his nose.

Yvonne Bacon was in heaven. Julian Greensleaves, the latest young actor-genius, had consented to sit for her. 'Do you strip well?' she had asked. 'Yes,' he had answered modestly. Beautiful *and* famous, my dear. Then there was old Cornelius, a *divine* old man. He had consented to sit for her, but she wasn't quite sure that he perfectly understood her. He had pinched really too hard. Beyond a joke. Then she saw Pat Barrington and introduced everybody to everybody. Harry Bartatt, the Yorkshire sculptor, and bald, fretful Eric Wetley clothed entirely in rubber, and Henry

74

Brewer the American genius. There was no other way of describing Brewer. Such a lovely lot of people! So amusing too: the six Celtic anarchists, the three exiled ladies from New York, the exclusive Laceys, Bernard Berkeley. *And more coming!* A pity about that dull little group in the corner. Still, they were famous too.

Wyndham Snowden, the leader of the younger poets, sat owlishly smoking a cigar, the loud bow-tie awry on his dirty collar. He never spoke. His white, spotty face was Buddhalike in its superiority, but the eyes behind the thick lenses didn't miss much. With him sat nice, donnish, middle-aged Edmund Bell. He didn't like talking either. His kind countryman's face showed absorption. He was composing a sonnet to be called 'Tree Creepers in Dymmock Park'. Fergus O'Hara sat with them because it hadn't occurred to him to sit anywhere else. There did not seem to be many other Jews in the party. He despised them all, and himself more than any.

More and more people were arriving. St John's station party; Hercules Jones and his stooge; old Magda Crawshay with Owen Tudor and Tom Agard; Roger Rashleigh, drinking champagne and dreaming of the revolution; sad Oliver Fry.

Cornelius suddenly broke into a roar. He seized Pat Barrington, and, unwittingly, avenged Christopher Garvin. The smack shook her to her foundations.

'You're a swell dame, baby, I could fall for you.'

She backed away for the first time in her life. The Nobel prize-winner followed her. Pat Barrington broke into a run, bowling over Basil Minto, sending Bill Dudley flying, with two hundred and fifty pounds of Nordic genius snorting behind her. She was saved by the luncheon gong.

Robin Shelley heard the gong on the terrace where she

was leaning her head against the kindly stone. 'Just another of them,' she thought. 'Damn and damn and damn.'

St John heard it, too, in the distant bathroom where he was scrubbing furiously. The towels were red with rouge.

The kitchens were packed with new servants getting in one another's way, asking one another where the Gold Room was or the Blue Room or the billiard-room, rushing with drinks to the library where Gordon still argued with Gill, or taking ice and poultices, sandwiches, umbrellas, newspapers, to weekend guests on the other floors. Rosemary and Mavis helped prepare the salads in Mrs Evans's private kitchen.

'I hope Mr Corbie's going to stay again,' Mavis said. 'Isn't this funny stuff to put in the salad? I've never seen it before. Where did it come from, Rosemary?'

'Mr Byrd brought it in specially. He says only to put it in the bowls on the foreign gentleman's table. The one who called you Sugar. I bet it's to make them sick.'

'You mustn't say that, Rosemary. Wouldn't it be wonderful? Or perhaps it's for worse than getting sick. Oh, dear.'

They cut the herbs into neat, small strips and sprinkled them over the lettuce.

Mr Ferney was acting waiter for the day, after the unfortunate incident of the sloe gin and one of the men brought down from London. He was smoking a cigarette he had taken from one of the many boxes on the dining-room side table. It was the nicest cigarette he had ever smoked. It made him very fast on his feet, and very small. Feeling no larger than the least of the Mr Hartleys, he raced about the kitchens like a whippet.

'Where's your boy friend, Rosemary? Has he called to see you yet?'

'He's not my boy friend, don't be a goose. He's a visitor: he won't come down to the kitchen again. He isn't interested. I know he isn't. Any reason why you think he should be, Mavis Woolston?'

'Oh, none at all, of course. No reason in the world, Miss Innocent. He only just came down to the kitchen a hundred times last weekend. Just every hour, that's all. I suppose he came down to see Mrs Evans.' Mavis stopped teasing. 'Oh, dear, if that was true,' she said, 'wouldn't it be wonderful?' She saw herself surprising an intimate scene between young Mr Ponting, guest and poet, and old Mrs Evans, the spreading cook.

'It isn't true at all,' said Rosemary angrily. 'You've got the nastiest mind of anybody I ever knew.' She remembered Captain St John, the terrible painted soldier with the hack-knife and the warning note, and she hurried on: 'And I hope Mr Corbie the magician turns you into something. There. Tomorrow morning when you take up his breakfast. I had a look in his room just now. He's got a coffin under the bed.'

'Go on, you fibber,' said Mavis delighted. 'He couldn't turn me into anything, could he? Could he?'

'May I come in and sit down,' asked Albert Ponting at the door. 'Just for a moment? I didn't have any breakfast.'

Mavis nudged Rosemary. 'Come in, sir, it's a pleasure,' she said. She looked him up and down. No, no, not him. He wouldn't provide the lovely scenes she wished to witness again: the elaborate seduction, the fight in the lavatory, the chase around the lily pond. What a shame Mr Spencer had been taken away. She had read the report in the *News of the World*. 'Man with Rod and Trident Arrested in Belgravia.' What had become of Mrs Enge? she wondered, that deep sleeper.

'Shall I get you the raspberry jam, Mr Ponting?' Rosemary's eyes were shining. He had come, he had come, like a prince from under the sea. 'Or the seedcake, Mr Ponting?' He had come to see her before anyone else. 'There's a big lump of ginger,' she said.

Mavis went out with the salads. Mr Ferney, his head reeling with speed, dragged after her.

During his little meal of home-made jam, seedcake, ginger and weak tea, Ponting tried several times to understand his reasons for coming to the kitchen almost straight away when the wildest party of the year was about to begin. Or had begun already, for hilarious shouting echoed from the hall. Did he want the jam very badly? Not very badly, though it was always nice. And seedcake was better than caviare any day. But he knew that why he had run down the servants' corridor, run as though there was not a moment to waste, was to see this blonde, plump parlourmaid, Rosemary, who stood now staring at him with her bright, brown eyes and playing with the strings of her apron. This could not, at any rate, be love; love was dark and cruel, biting as snakes or fires; if he fell in love it would be with an unsmiling woman with black, writhing hair. Love hurt you. This smiling young woman made you warm. You wanted to do soft, natural things and not suffer at all. He looked up.

'Oh, Mr Ponting, it's lovely to see you again,' Rosemary said.

There was nobody listening. He moved away from the table and stood near to her.

'I've got to go away now,' he said. 'I've got to get back to the party.'

Eight hired waiters, led by Mr Porson the butler, marched through the small kitchen. Mr Porson had been drilling them all the morning. Temporary, perhaps, they were still an army of eight footmen as in the great dead days of Dymmock hospitality and extravagance. It was good to have a little army back, if only for a day. Mr Porson marched them out as though to military music.

'I'll have to be with the others all the time now. Can I see you tonight?' Ponting did not care any more for the fatal women waiting him somewhere in the cruel night world. He said, 'Please will you meet me?'

Rosemary, all at once, became practical and level-headed, a woman of the world, who knew exactly what she could offer and what she could do. This young man was pleading for more than a date. It was an assignation. She liked him very much indeed. He was not a visitor nor a poet nor a prince, but only a shy boy who wanted to be with her. 'Eleven o'clock,' she said. 'Outside the back kitchen. On the steps. You must go now, go on, hurry.' As he went out, she said: 'Eleven. Sharp, mind.'

He walked along the corridor, wondering what he had begun, up the backstairs towards the clamour which rose as he pushed through the green baize door, braced for the world which fascinated and repelled him. That loathsome old satyr Cornelius – only think that back in Walton he had all his works in the Collected Edition – was chasing Mrs Barrington round the hall. Ponting stood, horrified, as Porson banged away at the gong. Cornelius was corralled in a corner and calmed down, while the others passed into the darkened, candlelit dining hall.

By a whim of Dominic Byrd's, this was cruciform, making as it were four tables. Each one of these was built to seat six a side: and there was an extra seat at the head of each cross-piece. Every branch of the great table thus seated thirteen. It was full today: Hilary Byrd had fifty-one guests. He sat down at the main head of the board, his back to the vast fireplace; at the three subordinate tableheads, each with his back to a separate vast fireplace, sat Atkins, Cornelius, and Hercules Jones.

Atkins had Lady Crystal Lacey at his right hand and Mona Boylan at his left.

Cornelius and Jones each had a pair of nameless ladies. They did not seem to need names.

Hilary had Robin Shelley and Lucretia Lacey.

The few remaining women were planted judiciously up and down the tables.

The feast began.

CHAPTER FIVE

THE CANARY SINGS

ROGER RASHLEIGH sat between Mrs Barrington and a middle-aged woman with red hair. He had failed to catch her name – it sounded like Daisy of the Bells, but his hearing had never been good – and he wondered what kind of a lion or monster she could be. Could she be – though this was doubtful, for she ate and drank with a smacking, public enjoyment and winked and tapped her nose whenever any-one looked at her – a famous lady novelist? He could only think of Rose Macaulay and Sheila Kaye-Smith, and she was obviously neither of those.

'Extraordinary soup,' he said. 'Do you think it could be birds' nest?'

'Birds' nest, duckie?' Mrs Burgin pushed him. He slump-ed against Mrs Barrington, putting one arm around her to steady himself.

'*After* the soup,' Mrs Barrington whispered. She released his hold gently.

'Birds' nests are full of bits of twig and birds' eggs,' said Mrs Burgin, 'this is Heinz's tomato.'

Misconstrued by one lady and corrected by another, Roger went on to the next course. He did not care to ask his companions what they thought of the queer little crea-tures on their plates. To him, they looked horribly like mice.

'If you ask me,' said Mrs Burgin, 'what I've got on my plate is mice.'

'They're quite obviously small birds,' Roger assured her.

'You and your old birds.' Mrs Burgin raised her hand to give him another push.

'Impetuous!' Mrs Barrington whispered again as he clutched at her bare, padded arm. 'Can't you wait? Is it too hard?' She pressed her thigh against his. He saved himself from being cast to the other lady by clinging on to the tablecloth.

In the snug little steward's room four men put their feet up. Two bottles of Scotch – 'to go on with,' Rosemary had shyly explained – a York ham, a double Gloucester, 'and they were to ring if they wanted any more.' They picked their teeth and fondled their cameras. This was better than the opening of a public library; it was better than a slap-up funeral; it was all right.

'Funny sort of joint.'

'Not very home-y.'

'Whisky's OK.'

'Fill mine up, will you, Charlie?'

'Rum sort of beggar.'

'Which one?'

'That's a good one.'

'Wonder how the girls are getting on?'

They got a plan of the table.

'Two of them's sitting on each side of old Hercules Jones.'

'That's a good one!'

'And the other two's sitting on each side of old Cornelius.'

'What, the old beggar we shot in the Carlton last week?'

'Phew!'

'That's a good one!'

At the head of his table J. L. Atkins tried to feel at ease. It was pleasant enough to have Lady Crystal at his right, but beyond her sat a tall young man – was the name

Gordon? – who seemed the worse for liquor, and beyond him again a crazy-looking creature. Oliver Fry, they called him. Then, it was scarcely good taste to put Miss Boylan on his left. She would insist upon discussing American writers of whom he had never heard; and, worse, cross-questioning him with gross impertinence about himself. He had long since laid Boston, and did not like the ghost to be raised.

Mallow, between Mona and Wyndham Snowden, was not enjoying himself, either. It was not his period. Ask him to show you the dent where Lionel Johnson's head hit the floor; the authentic cabman's shelter used by Dowson; apocrypha of Corvo; Middleton's spectacle-case; Arthur Machen's tobacco-jar: well and good. But Oliver Fry's would-be hypnotic stare, and Snowden's scornful silence, and an occasional verbal jab from Mona, kept him in the locked present. Perhaps he could get Atkins to sign his firsts. He didn't like them, but possessed them as a matter of course.

'Excuse me, Mr Atkins,' he leant forward, 'I wonder if, as one man of letters to another, I might . . .'

'Say, what is this, a literary lunch in Ithaca? Listen to this guy, will you?'

Atkins shuddered, and turned from them with a murmured apology to Crystal Lacey, with whom he'd been discussing eighteenth-century receipts for making rosewater.

'Young Rashleigh's trying to wreck the place already. See him tugging at the tablecloth? Typical modern manners. Can't hold their liquor. Destructive pup,' said Sir Frank Knight to his pretty, anonymous neighbour. He looked at the small, skinny shapes on the plate before him. If he hadn't known Byrd's father, he'd have thought that they were ... With a shudder he put the thought by him. 'These little fowl,' he said, 'remind me of the humming birds D'Annunzio and I used to have together in Fiume.'

The dark young woman smiled at him sweetly. Bore and liar. 'Was that in Italy?' she asked.

Placing a fatherly hand on the back of her chair, he explained.

The wingless birds lay uneaten.

Hercules Jones looked with a bloodhound's noble disdain at the mess before him. He beckoned to the servant. 'Take this disgusting offal away and bring me some bread-and-cheese.' The man carried away whatever they were in aspic, trembling.

Jones stared at Derek Gill, who was nervously trying to swallow the food; Tudor had slipped his under the table. The lovely blondes helped the great man. One to brandy, one to soda. This had been demanded very early on. Appeased, Jones leaned towards one as he pinched the other.

'When are you going to seduce me?' His whisper was like tearing calico.

'Dirty old man,' said Yvonne Bacon. She had known Jones for thirty years, but he had not spoken to her for twenty.

Tudor, opposite Gill, between one of the blondes and Prudence Whittier, helped himself again from one of the exotic salad bowls. He was conscious of a general euphoria. Yvonne's raddled face over the table seemed full of mysterious charm, and his neighbours were full of a charm quite unmysterious.

Farther down the table Humbert Jonas, scraggy as a plucked fowl, laid down the law to Henry Page and Bernard

Berkeley. Page looked worn and ill-at-ease; they were always bringing him new manifestos to sign. At the moment he was Catholic, a surrealist, a communist, an abstractionist, a pacifist, a rationalist, a social creditor, an anarchist and a nudist. People were beginning to accuse him of insincerity: an unfounded charge, as he believed passionately in his signature. Now Jonas had worked round from Brancusi's egg to the idea of a world state based on what he called negativism.

Bernard Berkeley's nose twitched like a hare's. All Balliol in his voice: 'Do you *really* think so, Mr Jonas?' crumbling bread, the neat, thin head on one side.

'Ah doan't quite get that, Hoombert,' said Bartatt, England's greatest sculptor, solid as one of his works.

'It was all exploded by Zempler when I was in Paris in 1913,' Tommy Brock defending his period.

Ostler backed him up. 'I was there too. I can remember Strindberg discussing the esoteric aspect of the matter with Bergson and . . .'

'Are you from Yorkshire, too?' said Bartatt friendlily, leaning across Page in his enthusiasm.

'I was *born* there,' said Ostler haughtily.

Jonas gabbled on: '. . . and the refusal to adopt a positive results in this *lovely* vacuum – it's all in Lao Tze. . . .'

Magda Crawshay, sitting on Sir Frank's left-hand side, ate everything and without looking. She downed the mice with hock. She followed the hock with Sir Frank's double whiskey. He saw her drinking it, and elbowed his plate towards her. 'D'Annunzio showed me his poems to La Duse, nobody else had ever . . .' Yes, the sacrifice of the whiskey was worth it. Magda Crawshay ate, with enjoyment, a second helping. 'You're an Egyptian,' she told Julian Greensleaves.

'You're an old *bore*,' said Eric Wetley. He had had a great deal to eat and drink, and his indiarubber suit was extremely uncomfortable.

Henry Brewer paid no attention. His polysyllabic hunks of autobiography went on tumbling obscenely over one another.

Limpet, most famous of unsuccessful young composers, tried to calm Wetley down, but he began throwing things at the inexorable seven-day bicyclist's voice.

Lord Lacey looked on with distaste. His neighbours were neither of them congenial. He preferred Hodgson's tykesy jauntiness to Corbie's obscene bulk, but he knew he was being talked into a bust. It was always happening. The upper rooms at Lacey were full of the fruits of his kind heart and inherited gift of patronage. A man of taste might as well be deaf and blind in this vulgar age, he thought sadly. Opposite him Sidney Gorman gobbled and glowered. That Captain St John looked more tolerable, and quite white with boredom. Sympathetic. At the head of the table horrible Hilary attended to his sister Lucretia and the Shelley girl, with a crossfire from Basil Minto and Tom Agard. Really, some of the words that appalling American was pouring out!

'You are an old *bore*,' screamed Wetley again.

Ponting thought of Rosemary as he tried to forget the second course. Was she eating those things in the kitchen too, or were they delicacies only for the guests? He thought how nice it would be in the kitchen, having proper food. That waiter over there was behaving very queerly, moving from table to table like a tortoise. He took nearly a minute to put a new salad bowl before Cornelius. Ponting counted the seconds.

86

'Say something to me,' Sadie Lowenstein said. 'I'm bored. Do you think Pat Barrington really is a pathological case? She used to have a glorious body. And the lovers! Well!'

'I don't know Mrs Barrington intimately. I knew she was rather special, of course. Rubens with a touch of . . .' No painter came to his mind.

'With a touch of Havelock Ellis,' Sadie said, 'you can take my word.'

'Have you noticed that waiter?'

'Not too bad. A trifle coarse, but definitely a body.' She eyed him all over. 'He'd need a bit of polishing, but I think I could make him work.'

'No, no. I mean have you noticed how slow he is. Look, he's like a sonnambulist.'

'He could walk in my sleep okay.' Full of ideas, she turned to Julian Greensleaves.

'Come, not an Egyptian, Mrs Crawshay,' he was saying.

'An Egyptian mummy,' Mrs Crawshay said. 'Tut somebody, that's who you are. I know it by your skin,' she shouted.

'He certainly has got a perfect skin,' Sadie said, 'have a look at that peach blossom. Wouldn't little Sadie give a couple of dollars to have a complexion like that.' She raised her blotched, white face to his, invitingly.

'You could give the Lowenstein millions,' Mrs Crawshay said, 'and you'd still look like poison ivy.'

'Did you ever see that Easter Island sculpture of the woman with the . . .?' Sadie asked Greensleaves.

In silence Mrs Crawshay waited for the insult, her arms folded, her large foot, in football stocking and broken side-boot, ready to avenge.

Bill Dudley looked across at Edmund Bell. He felt sick,

but Bell munched on, an abstract look in his eyes. Tree creepers were such gay little chaps.

Next to them, Fergus O'Hara, the Irish Jew, was acutely embarrassed at finding himself next to Mahaffy and opposite the equally unsettling anarchist O'Brien. O'Brien was sitting between Dudley and Sigismund Gold, who was even less at ease. Fergus O'Hara and himself were being subjected to an unfair attack. They had studiously avoided having met, and now they were lumped together and mocked at as if they were secret allies. It was indeed difficult to tell them apart.

'I suppose you're an Irishman too,' said Mahaffy, with heavy irony, across the table.

'Alas, no. I have visited your lovely unhappy country, with love for its beauty, being a poet, and for its woes, belonging myself to an ancient and persecuted race.'

O'Hara blushed as O'Brien, replying, fixed him with a bloodshot eye. 'An' who made it unhappy, by God? The English came first and the Jews came after the English, and they've bled the country white between them.'

'We shouldn't be too hard on the English,' said O'Hara, as it were in defence of Dudley and Bell.

'*We*, who said *we*?' demanded O'Brien, as Mahaffy tittered noiselessly.

'Came of a very old Boston family. A pupil of William James.'

'Say, don't listen to all that old stuff, lady. Get him to tell you about the time they set fire to the Select. Boy, was that a party! A liberal education. Never mind about Harvard – let Harvard worry.'

'I think overeating's disgusting,' Ponting said. The little birds, or bats, or lizards, had almost disgraced him: one more thin, soft bone or slinky mouthful of sweet flesh and he would have had to leave the table. He might even have been asked to leave.

The man on the other side of the table, wearing a singed sports jacket, was too busy to answer.

'I don't think I like swan,' Ponting said. This was worse than he had expected. On his right, Magda Crawshay and Sadie Lowenstein, two dreadful women, one obscenely thin, one old and swollen, hissed and shouted at each other; that actor Greensleaves was entreating them to be 'friendly girls' in a nervous but always modulated voice; Sir Frank Knight described Tagore to a young woman who was not listening. And at the head of the table, Cornelius, his favourite modern author until that afternoon, was going down on all fours under the table and crawling among the legs. 'I think swan's awful, don't you?' Ponting said. He wouldn't look at Cornelius. He would write an essay to be called 'The Myth of Cornelius'. He'd tell Mother to put all Cornelius's tragedies in the boxroom along with Maeterlinck and Henty and *The Hill* and *Under the Hill* and *Tell England* and *Dolores*.

The man in the sports jacket spluttered an answer. What could 'frush' and 'whample' mean? The foreigner leant his elbow in Ponting's salad. ''A like whuskey an' 'a like pug,' McManus said.

'Yes, I'll sign.' In spite of Bartatt's sense, and the scorn of Brock and Ostler, in spite of Berkeley's Balliol incredulity, he would sign. Jonas was so plausible, and the idea was so attractive, after all it might be true. Truth, that was the thing. 'Yes, of course I'll sign,' Page repeated.

'No, not an archaeologist, an *architectural journalist*.'
'An anthropologist? Aesthetics and anthropology – the

only sciences. I suppose Burma's *most interesting*? A very rich field.' He leered like Silenus, winked at his neighbours.

Derek Gill cursed Gordon. He'd always wanted to meet Hercules Jones, and now that misleading introduction had messed the whole thing up. He gulped a glass of champagne, and began talking wildly, desperately.

Mr Ferney moved from guest to guest. That was the best cigarette in the world. Boy, am I whizzing! He felt so small and swift that he decided to cut short his journey to the kitchen by darting under the table. Very slowly and dreamily he lifted the cloth and disappeared.

'Whassa time?'

'Nearly six.'

'Pussha bell again, Corky.'

Four full photographers looked at three empty whiskey bottles.

The door opened and Rosemary stood holding on to the handle. She wasn't going to let happen what had happened last time. Dirty pigs.

'Atta girl.'

'Oh, baby.'

'Hello, sugar.'

Corky didn't say anything. He was slumped in the corner by the bell.

'Bring's another bottla whisky, honey.'

Drink gave the cockney voices the necessary tough touch. Rosemary fled.

'Let's have some air.'

'Look out – Jack's put his head through the window.'

'Put him down.'

'Give him some whisky.'

'Don't let him bleed on the table.'

'Pusha bell, Corky.'

Corky began to snore.

Just as Christopher Garvin was telling himself that nothing could make the afternoon more intolerable, he felt two hands on his knees. He sat quite still, waiting for the last embarrassment. The hands moved slowly up. They were nearly there. 'Oh, don't please, Mrs Barrington.' He could stand it no longer.

'I'm not doing anything, silly boy,' Mrs Barrington said.

The hands were reaching towards his waist. He rapped them across the knuckles with the salad spoon, but they clung on. He looked round wildly. Cornelius was in sight, for once, pulling the nameless young woman towards him by her beads.

'Mrs Barrington, Mrs Barrington, there's something between my legs.'

Before she had time to answer, a large, bald head appeared.

Yvonne Bacon, the two blonde ladies, even Hercules Jones, were impressed. Mr Gill – Gull? – had seemed such a quiet little man, too. Of course, the tropics affected people in very odd ways, but rarely in such very odd ways as these.

'. . . the boys, and after the initiation ceremonies were over we went into the Place of Women, just myself and the Priest, and . . .'

'Have some more of these,' whispered Owen Tudor, his hands dabbling in the salad bowl. His eyes were shining in an altogether compelling manner. Prudence Whittier reached out her hand again.

'. . . didn't come out until the rains were over. I suppose it was the mo-mo root that kept one going.'

'The mo-mo root?'

'Yes. Red phallic-shaped root with a curious white flower. Only grows every seventh spring. That's another interesting ceremony. All the girls who have reached puberty since the last rites go out with the old women to search for the root, and one of them always fails to return. Of course, it's a matrilinear society and the secrets are all in the hands of the women and the hereditary high priest. Luckily for me, I was able to be of some use to the man, and he told me the whole thing. As a matter of fact, I *saw* the whole thing.'

He told them about it. The lies which came so fluently invigorated him. His own mother would not have recognized him; and what she would have thought of his story it is impossible to conceive. It was strange indeed: the result of thirty years' pure imagination.

'What the devil's going on there? There's a fellow under the table. Can you see his head, m'dear? Beats me where they all come from. Here, there and everywhere, under the table, snuffling and barking. Unsettles a man.' Sir Frank was stern with his neighbours. 'No tact,' he said. 'Place for a fellow at lunch is on a chair, not gadding about your feet like a pariah dog.'

'It's the waiter,' Mrs Barrington cried out.

Mr Ferney stared into a strange waistcoat.

'Jack in de boxie,' said Cornelius. He offered salad to the head.

The occurrence at Cornelius's table passed unnoticed by most of the guests. Hilary Byrd, however, saw it from the beginning. Intrigued, all during luncheon, by Mr Ferney's trancelike gliding among the guests and plates, he waited calmly for some calamity to happen. He was pleased with the party: everyone was behaving as he wished. A chauffeur under the influence of drugs was a soundly grotesque addition. This was worth all the trouble of arranging a vast banquet to suit the tastes of few.

The luncheon plans he had drawn up in his Bluebeard's room were well rewarded by the spectacle of so many distinguished and notorious people sitting in uncongenial company: squabbling and sometimes coming to blows; bending in despair over the body of a doped waiter; full of erotic herbs, pawing and mauling; sick from mice, faint with swan; insulting, insulted; out of their depths or drowned in argument and excess.

The meal had cost nothing. St John had paid him a ridiculous amount of money for a dim Haydon in the outer hall. He looked at the Captain with gratitude. The military old tart had taken his make-up off. 'Would you lend the Captain your compact, Mr Minto?' he asked softly, and sat back to enjoy the scene.

'Don't be a bore, Hilary,' Robin Shelley said. 'Leave him alone.' Her face was pinched and tired; her fingers were not steady; she kept brushing back a lock of hair that fell over her forehead, and making the same movement even when the lock was in place. She passed her tongue over her lips.

St John, not listening to the talk around him, studied every detail of her face, the telltale trembling and the small sweat breaking out, the dilation of her eyes, the low-cut dress she wore with the sadly long sleeves.

'Look,' Hilary said in that same soft, insidious voice, 'they're carrying a waiter out. Poor fellow, he's an inveterate marijuana smoker. I only keep him on because he's my illegitimate brother, Lady Lucretia. I think drug-takers are so pitiable, don't you, Miss Shelley? However, their hair falls out, their teeth decay, their wits, my dear, go gathering. So young and so silly.'

'In Ecuador in the early fifteenth century,' said Tom Agard, who had been silent for too long, but only through necessity, for the claret had to be finished, 'the older priests were allowed by law to take, every fifth day in March, a certain flower dipped in holy crocodile water which had the most gratifying effects: they could speak through their navels.' He relaxed again; the massive chair creaked.

Lady Lucretia, interested, in spite of the indelicate phraseology, in all old customs, looked long and hard at Agard from under her lemon-coloured lashes.

> (*Veils of a lemon tree*
> *Over serenity*
> *Pale as peacocks the lashes dance,*

she had written in *Punch and Judy*.) The ponderous young man appeared sufficiently serious, though she could but notice that the claret was sinking in yet another decanter.

'In the *fifteenth* century? Are you sure, Mr Agard?' she asked.

'Mr Agard is always sure,' said Basil Minto, 'if not always correct. A scholar of opinions, Lady Lucretia.'

There was the noise of a man coming out of a pit: a wrenching and scraping, a rattle of chains in the throat: and Hamish Corbie, silent as the grave for two hours, released, slowly, the dust-dry torrents of his profound and unenviable wisdom. 'Man Aga Mem by the Seven Dams of Sheba's Toad,' he cried. 'In the thirteenth genital layer of the Sphinx a navel speaks through a priest dipped in night-shade. Logos Six Am. By Horus's last star. Yo, Yo,' making a cross of his arms.

Everyone at the table stopped quarrelling and stared at the Black Master. Ancient blessings and curses poured from

94

his lips. He clapped his huge hands in a forgotten rhythm, and brought out a glass ball from his pocket.

He looked like an absconding bank manager.

Hilary Byrd rose to his feet. Those who had taken, unwittingly, the marijuana cigarettes, puffed in silence and waited for a miracle. Their host had the gestures of lightning. His words came racing out. Those who had drunk too deeply noised and clapped according to their habits, some banging on the table, some crying 'Hear, hear' before a word had been spoken, some shouting 'Sit down', one or two whistling between their fingers; or sat in private jungles and counted the hosts. The polite paid grave attention: this was a day to remember in the history of literature. The bored and distressed sat still, alongside people they could never like, and waited for the very worst. The salad eaters thought of one thing. Those on the borderline of sanity or society nudged, fawned, mouthed, retired into neurosis. Hamish Corbie studied his ball. Cornelius hoped the speech would be short: he had a woman to catch.

'My Lords, Ladies, and Gentlemen,' said Hilary Byrd, 'I am proud today to speak to you as the sixteenth Poet Laureate of England, and a more unpopular choice than even Henry James Pye. Before me I see the flowers of English culture and intelligence. And out of all such vegetable glory *I* have been most favoured, by the intemperate selection of a gentleman who knew my father.'

'It's perfectly clear that Crewe was tight. Why mention it?' said Roger Rashleigh to Mrs Burgin.

'If he was tight and the Prime Minister himself I wouldn't let him in my public bar.'

'He *is* the Prime Minister.'

'Oh, I'd let him in the lounge bar, of course. You can do anything there.'

Across the table Sir Frank sneered gloomily. King Lear, that's what he was. His rightful kingdom divided amongst ungrateful children. It had come to this. An old man mocked, the whole establishment turning on a drunkard's whim, order gone from the land. Where were Mowbray, where Bohun, where Mortimer? His head was spinning with betrayal. The only man who could have saved the situation! And he sat, neglected and alone, a prey to reviewers and the young. He filled his glass. Thou wast not born for death, immortal bird!

'There can be no need now for me to discuss the nature of my appointment; its function is as dead as its dignitaries, and no one is the loser. In the past – God send it to a comfortable hell – the Poet Laureate was given a barrel of canary wine in which to drown his dusty muse or bury a sad, dead head crowned with dandruff and laurel. But glorious Pye, teetotaller and friend of worms, demanded money in the canary's place, and a custom was established, and the leagues of sterility and abstinence applauded the triumph of common nonsense. Today, as Unpious the Sixteenth, capped Knave of Poetry, I hold in my hand a hundred pounds. The King's Hangman, a servant of the Crown as I am, must needs break five spines for this. My work was easier. I parodied the poetry of my day, and broke my eggs on your heads.'

'A young man's wit.' Atkins was solicitous. 'My dear Lady Crystal, I'm sure the intention is innocent, even if the expression is unhappy.'

'He's just plain vicious, why wrap it up?'

'I think, Miss Boylan, we can scarcely judge of that.'

'I am inclined to agree with Miss Boylan. Mr Byrd's taste is execrable.'

'With this hundred pounds I have decided to present a number of gifts to deserving causes. Do not let it be said in the abhorrent days of tyranny and insipidity to come, that the successor of vast Southey and inspired Austin was an uncharitable man. I present:

'Item: To the Governors of the Bank of England, a skull and a pound of shot.

'Item: To the King's Hangman, a mirror.

'Item: To console St Dunstan's, a collage by Oliver Fry.'

Fry heard his name spoken aloud. He had been thinking of what Miss Boylan had called him before luncheon. 'A dead bird,' she had said. Birds were outworn. One did not paint them now, unless one added a cloven foot or drew the breast in the shape of a crab. He could not understand. He had always been *avant garde*. Birds were academic property. It was absurd to call him an academician. He believed passionately in his inability to draw.

'Did somebody call me something?' he asked Gordon.

Gordon, in a whisper, told him what Hilary had said.

'But St Dunstan's is a home for the blind.'

'That's what Hilary meant.'

And Hilary had once called him the Hope of the Depression!

It was a movement, not himself alone, that was being betrayed.

'Item: To the Prime Minister, six copies of my banned book, *An English Rose*.

'Item: To the Prison Reform Commission, a cat o' eight tails.

'Item: To the Wine and Food Society, the remnants and dregs of this meal.

'Item: To the Archbishop of Canterbury, a Guide to the Bahamas.

'Item: To the Licensed Victuallers' Benevolent Association, a snapshot of Sir Frank Knight walking down the Strand, three five p.m.

'Item: To the Girls' Friendly Society, a very curious Chinese paperweight.

'Item: To the British Legion, some assorted Great War medals, picked up in a pawnbroker's.

'Item: To Dr Barnardo's Homes, a gold-framed photograph of Lacey Hall.'

Lady Lucretia Lacey rose. Lady Crystal at the other end of the hall rose also. Their brother waited until his two pale sisters in brocaded dresses had glided to the door. Then he bowed to the company, sleeved his small lace handkerchief, and followed them. In the order of their ages they retired. Lord Lacey closed the door soundlessly. Hilary did not pause.

The Ladies Lacey trod the long hallway, two old gazelles, their delicate, pointed feet invisible, closed fans in their hands. Lord Lacey tiptoed behind them.

Content to let their turbans and summer capes remain forever in the evil house, the ladies moved to the doorway, waiting for their victoria to come through the empty courtyard.

Lord Lacey gathered his tall, white hat from the cloakroom. He called down the still, echoing corridors in a high voice that carried no distance at all: 'Quince, Quince, the horses.'

Their man did not appear, nor was Porson at his post. He was attending to a wounded man. The kitchens were naturally unapproachable.

The three Laceys stood by the lily pond, looking at the sun.

In the shunned dining hall Hilary Byrd went on:

'And now permit me voyage into the literary past. I do not propose to discuss my immediate predecessors; there are, I can assure you, limits even to my bad taste.'

He dropped into the easy gabble of the popular lecturer.

'The term "Laureate" was originally given to any distinguished poet. Skelton, Ben Jonson, and Davenant, for example. Or a great poet might be honoured by the King, as were Chaucer and Spenser; and, farther back, those mysterious figures Gulielmus Peregrinus, Master Henry, and John Kay. The first official Poet Laureate was John Dryden, and before the three Laureates who immediately precede myself were Wordsworth and Tennyson. Each of them, in his different fashion, a poet in some sort. It is in between Dryden and Wordsworth that we have the fine foolish line of balderdashers whom I am proud to follow. Sometimes I wonder why my bad verse should have been chosen in the teeth of such strong opposition. As I look round this room I can see so clearly many of you whose claim is even greater than mine, who may say, "I, or I, or I, have written more unutterable ostrobogulisms even than yourself. Mine should be the prize!" '

For a moment his words were lost in the hiss and cackle of offended poets.

'He means me most,' Tudor said proudly. 'Why is your skin so silky?'

'It's only because he doesn't understand what we're doing,' said Ponting to McManus. 'He told Basil that he hadn't read a *word* of poetry since 1939.'

'He couldn't understand a tiddler's bit of the best verse written today,' McManus said. 'It's all in Scotch.'

'Let us see how that might work out. After Dryden came Shadwell. How well Mr O'Hara could have matched his dreary odes! Then Nahum Tate, whom even Mr Gold might find it hard to rival in feeble cliché. Nicholas Rowe: who could compare with him? Good Mr Bell, I think. Laurence Eusden next, a dunderhead very dear to me. Of

99

him Gray said that "he was a person of great hopes in his youth but he turned drunken parson". Of him Pope wrote, "how Laurus lay inspired beside a sink". Only lively when bawdy, a master of bathos, this "excellent parson much bemused in beer" spent his literary life "uttering fulsome flattery in mediocre poetry". He died, and we may be sure Pope grieved as he wrote that "Eusden thirsts no more for sack or praise". I feel abashed that myself should have been chosen to succeed this glorious figure, when I see below me a man with every qualification save that he is not in holy orders: Sir Frank Knight.'

Even in the midst of his rage, Sir Frank, who was, after all, in Mallow's phrase, 'a man of letters', managed by a supreme effort of will to spare a thought for Eusden. He had edited Eusden for the Porthmeirion Society, and in his preface had suggested that the forgotten Poet Laureate was underrated. 'Eusden may lack the passion of Keats, the profundity of Coleridge, the glitter of Pope, but he had the root of the matter in him.' Let poetasting puppies do their worst, Eusden and Knight would shock them!

'Then Cibber, grotesque Cibber; and William Whitehead the irreproachable. Why not our friend Mallow for one, and Mr Atkins for the other. Warton? You, I think, Gordon. And that prince of bores Henry James Pye, whose work was a continual "source of contempt"; who "read and wrote assiduously but who was destitute of any power of expression"; who was "eminently respectable in everything but his poetry"; whom even Southey could afford to despise. Christopher Garvin: surely you are his legitimate heir?'

Mrs Burgin whispered to Roger Rashleigh: 'That's one for his nob.' Christopher Garvin had been introduced to her only an hour before. Seeing in her another, and an even less inhibited, Pat Barrington, he had not dared to shake her hand, but had dived his own under his coat and backed away.

'Don't let it worry you, Kit dear,' Pat Barrington said in a husky voice, 'you've got more than your poetry. Much, much more.'

'Worried? Really, the whole thing's a scream. I wouldn't miss it for worlds.'

He wished he were dead.

'Southey? I leave you to elect your own Southey. Shall it be Albert Ponting? Perhaps I myself will do, after all.

'Yes, let us not condemn my appointment too harshly. I look from this table at my friends and rivals. What do I see? You write as badly as the little men I named. That is your only claim to distinction. You dare to speak of art and poetry who have failed even to be elected to the Fool's throne I find myself upon. What do you know of these or any other things? Seventeen alcoholics, seventeen versifiers, thirteen snobs and social climbers, thirteen plain bores, seven anarchists, seven dope-fiends, seven assorted perverts, seven nymphomaniacs, seven pathics, seven ordinary lunatics: one hundred and two attributes for fifty-one people. How lucky you are! Some of you must share two or more of these delightful qualities. Perhaps I share more than any of you. I feel emboldened to give your toast: the new Poet Laureate!'

At a sign from his master, old Porson opened a door, and in the midst of the chatter of fury three figures, one with a blood-stained handkerchief round his head, ran crazily into the room. What they saw sobered even their fuddled heads. This was News! With hands shaking more from excitement than from alcohol, they aimed their cameras, and aimed again.

Hilary posed before the magnesium flashes. He put on the entranced expression of a man of destiny scanning the horizon; he even went so far as to shade his eyes with his hand like an Indian scout. Then, without warning, and to the bewilderment and delight of the unsteady photographers, he changed his stance completely and stood on tiptoe, scattering invisible flowers like a Spring Song dancer, simpering, blowing kisses. And once again he changed, this time grotesquely: he bowed his back, raised one shoulder higher than the other, and made such a distorted and obscene face that the three photographers reeled back.

'Snap that one, Charlie.'

'There's a puss.'

'Mr Poet Laureate, Mr Poet Laureate, do us another gorilla.'

'Here comes Corky. Look at the Poet Laureate, Corky.'

The Laureate was standing on the table, blowing kisses again.

'Gee,' Corky said.

'Run down to the end of the table, Charlie, I just saw old Cornelius.'

'Look at him.'

'Who's on his back?'

'Gee!'

'It's little Phyllis Constant from the *Standard*.'

'And there's Cousin Faithful sitting on a boozer's knee. Got 'em, Charlie?'

The nameless young women had been very clever indeed, but their profession was not what Cornelius and Hercules Jones had imagined.

The photographers staggered from one sensation to another. Few guests appeared to notice them in the mix-up. Some retired wildly, not caring how they got out so long as they did, knocking over chairs, dislodging the weak;

some, in corners, wrestled over problems; some were led away; others succumbed; all argued at the top of their voices.

'Infernal impudence.'

'Man's a madman.'

'Let me get at him.'

'Somebody hit Sidney.'

'He said I was a nymphomaniac.'

'Who hit Sidney?'

'So you are.'

'For God's sake let's get away.'

'Damned pup.'

'There's a lady on the floor.'

'The most ill-mannered exhibition.'

'Why is he pretending to be a hunchback?'

'Really, may I be allowed to reach the door?'

'It isn't pretty.'

'*Seven* lunatics!'

'Say, he's crazy as a senator.'

'Oh, do be friendly, dears.'

'The beast, the beast!'

'Remarkable study in repressed . . .'

'Used to love a horse.'

'He, he, Basil's down.'

'Wouldn't have missed this.'

'You old *bore*!'

'He's made a mock of the whole . . .'

The Press moved in an orgy of violence and scandal, their heads full of two-inch type, and the young women under false pretences would remember everything.

From the courtyard they could hear the din rising in the hall; and to it was now added a cracking of whips, a howling of beasts and a rattle of wheels. Would Quince never come?

The Laceys recoiled as the first of several motor-caravans crashed through the great gateway and into the courtyard. Faces peered from the windows – animal and human; and some betwixt and between, of giants and pigmies, shrivelled or swollen. The most finely tempered nerves could not face this new horror. For the first time in history a Lacey ran.

CHAPTER SIX

BIRD'S EYE VIEW

NOTHING had been removed from the tables, except some expensive forks. The carcasses of the swans resembled half-built boats. Mice remained on many plates. Spilt wine mirrored the silverware. Glass was splintered, and an ashtray placed upside down where a poet had failed to understand. Blood stained a discarded napkin. A strong novelist at the other end of the room had torn up a pack of cards and scattered it like confetti. In a corner was a pool, and on the chair that had seated an architect fond of salad lay a heap of clothing. The hall reeked of magnesium. In the distance hyenas spoke, lions replied, the Suffolk summer evening grew loud with the conversation of the Wild.

Hilary Byrd sat alone, grave and still. His face, in repose, suggested an impersonal calm. The guests of an hour before would not have recognized that monastic mask. All anger, mischief, and perversion had faded from it. Colourless eyes contemplated the identities of shadows falling across the ravaged tables and filling the chairs; the hands were folded; the thin lips moved without sound. He might have been saying a grace after meat.

'From what we have eaten, may the Lord preserve us,' he said to the company gone. He had taken neither aphrodisiac nor narcotic.

He was the witness against his guests. His head must be cool and his nerves silent. The others should rage and chase, be sick, topple down, lust without want, leak out their secrets, committing to his memory alone the crimes and follies of the famous day and the extravagant night to come.

His enemies were moving towards an end, and he would be there: helping the weak to break, the foolish to surpass, the feeble and vicious ladies and gentlemen of the underworld of the intellect finally to proclaim themselves. This was the first day of a prodigious new career. The old house, undisturbed too long, hissed and bubbled around him. In every room, men and women behaved as they were meant. There was not one who did not hate or despise him: the precise insult, the proper clownishness, the intonation of each exaggerated sneer, had taken a long time to calculate and perfect. Now the drunk were growing drunker, the lustful scrabbled and fell, senility drivelled in the locked bedrooms, talk talk the flat horror of talk behind closed doors. On the syringes, the bottles, the whips, the lipsticks, the hate and concupiscence and masterly silliness in the house. He celebrated the rebirth of Dymmock by raising a glass of water to the assembled shadows. The last puritan of his line. Then he rose, wiped his fingers carefully on a napkin, and went out to inspect.

He noticed with surprise that the door leading to the chapel was open. He peeped inside. Looking like three Chartres figures, the Laceys sat, frozen. They must have been there for hours, he thought.

'Ah, Mr Byrd, we could not find any responsible person to ask for the carriage. Will you request your servant to find my coachman? There did not seem to be anyone to help us, and the courtyard is full of wild beasts and gypsies.'

'Oh, that's just the fairing,' said Hilary. 'I asked them all up today to round off the occasion. You'll enjoy the show.'

Lady Crystal had written a history of Clowns called *Fard and Fanfare*.

'We prefer not to stay, Mr Byrd.'

'But you must. I insist.'

'We prefer not to stay.'

'I'll find your man, then, and tell him where you are. That is, if you are going to stay in the Chapel.'

'Will anybody else be coming here?'

'It's extremely unlikely.'

'Then we prefer to stay where we are.'

He left them in their thirteenth-century elongated frigidity and walked towards the house.

He went into the library. Good. Everyone there was a bore. Everyone was thick of speech. Sir Frank lay asleep on a couch. Gordon, who could hardly speak, was speaking most. Hercules Jones was requesting the young woman whose profession he was sure of to sit for him in the country.

'In a dress, naturally. In a low dress. No dress. No dress, naturally, I paint flesh and bone. Flesh and bone. Hallo, come in, take a pew. I've just been talking to our friend Gill here about the new diggings. Remarkably interesting.' He pinched the Editress of the Woman's Page.

Gordon, invisible in the deep armchair he always occupied at Dymmock, raised his glass into sight. 'Now, Burma old boy, tell Hilary about all the women you found in the mummy cases.'

'In the mummy cases?' Derek Gill stammered.

'You remember. That night you were in the tomb. You told us about it at dinner. Your memory's going, old boy. Shouldn't drink. Play more squash.' The glass disappeared.

'They were Dravidian,' Derek Gill said wildly, 'and one of them was brachycephalic. It was very late at night, of course, and we'd been digging for hours and I had a lot of vases and the professor had found a sarcophagus full of . . .' He looked to Hilary for help; Hilary smiled and nodded – 'full of papyrus and burins.'

'Remarkable period,' Hercules Jones said, frowning with

attention, 'I shall look forward to your monogram.' He paused. 'Monograph.'

'Tell me, Burma, how do you manage to get around so much?' asked the voice from the deep chair. 'I always understood you were the architectural expert of *Hill and Dale*. Pretty expensive hobby, archaeology. No architecture in Burma. Only teak.'

'I'd like you to sit for me, Mr Gill, when you're not on a dig. On a digging. Perhaps I could paint you in a topee, eh?'

'Beats me what an architect wants to wear a topee for.'

Hilary trod unnoticed out of the room.

'I'm not an architect, I'm an anthropologist,' he heard Derek Gill cry out shrilly as he shut the door.

That couldn't have been better. The complications were piling up. Soon nobody in the library would know who he was, and then Sir Frank would awake.

Hilary entered a small room decorated as a Victorian bar parlour, and found Roger Rashleigh conducting a poker game.

'I don't see how you can have a full house, Mrs Burgin, when you've only got three cards,' Roger said. 'How do, Hilary, care for a hand?'

'Thank you, no. I'm just on a little tour.'

'My house is always full,' said Mrs Burgin loudly. 'The Four Bells. Halifax's.' She picked up the kitty.

'No, no, Mrs Burgin, this is poker, you must abide by the rules.'

'You and your old rules, they're as bad as birds with you. Mr O'Brien owes me one and fourpence.'

'You're the devil herself, Mrs B.'

Mahaffy said, slyly, 'Five kings. My game. You owe me a pound.'

'How can you have five kings when I've got one?'

'Because we're using two packs.'

'There's only one pack on the table.'

'Here's the other, look for yourself.' Mahaffy produced it.

'Didn't you speak like a bastard after luncheon,' said O'Brien in a friendly voice. 'I'd have murdered you if you'd touched my name with your lying tongue.'

Roger dealt wearily.

'Full house, full house,' Mrs Burgin cried. She was look-ing at the backs of her five cards.

'Going? Can't blame you. No, Mrs Burgin, the other way round. Please, Mrs Burgin, for my sake. As a personal favour, it's nothing to do with the rules, really. Oliver Fry's looking for you, Hilary, and Sir Frank and Kit Garvin, oh, the whole troupe.'

'You'll be getting a long bed.'

'And he can lie in it.'

Mahaffy was cheating quietly, and the cries of his dis-coverers followed Hilary along the corridor towards the music room.

Better and better. The Irish were angry, the artists were hunting, he was glad he had invited Mrs Burgin. They would be fighting soon, reckless, stupid, half-mad anarchists with nothing better to offer the rotting world than the liberation of individual fools, and worse. A world with Mahaffy sneering and cheating coldly through it, callous, lawless, friendless, his own corrupt government and king! It was a prospect that made him turn, almost with gratitude, to the thick bellow of Sir Frank Knight behind him.

'Ah, Sir Frank, up and lively as ever after your nap?' He smiled with such sudden archness that Sir Frank was unnerved.

'Wanted to see you,' Sir Frank mumbled, 'tell you you're not worthy to be' – his voice trailed away before Hilary's head-cocked smile, then rumbled to life again as the old fumes rose up and his eyes grew bloodshot – 'the son of your father. Austin Byrd was a man, every inch of him. You're a literary cheapjack, Byrd. Shouldn't be allowed in a decent club. Deeply regret having broken your bread. If I were ten years younger . . .'

'You'd be eleven years further from the grave. Are you coming my way, to the music room, Sir Frank? There may be some whisky under the harpsichord.'

The harpsichord was being played, very loudly, as Hilary entered. For a moment he could not see where it was. Porson was always moving the furniture, a habit acquired from a lifetime's service under Sir Austin whose hobby was ghost-foiling. Towards the end of his life he moved from room to room, baffling poltergeists and elementals, barricading himself against protoplasmata, artfully disguising the appearance of each room. The music room had been the old man's last refuge, and every so often Porson would go through the ritual as though his master were still alive.

The harpsichord was not where it had last been, but the reason for its invisibility was largely due to the black bulk of Tom Agard, who was seated at the keyboard, his back to the door. He finished the Goldberg Variations.

'And now we'll have some Couperin: *Les Fastes de la grande et ancienne Menestrandise*. In your honour, sirs.'

He bowed towards his audience – a row of heads at different heights peering through the open windows.

Hilary sat beside Robin Shelley and Captain St John. The music, first grave and then fantastic, flowed over them. The heads of the tattooed lady, the giant, the Siamese twins wagged to the unfamiliar rhythm. Disappointed at first by the incongruous beauty of the music, Hilary took comfort at the absurdity of the audience. At the end, too, as he rose to go, Robin Shelley's 'Thank God you're going' had the authentic furious note. More faces appeared at the window.

One of them had a beard. Six of them barely reached the sill. Agard began the Cats' Fugue of Scarlatti.

Albert Ponting was leaning, as though lost, against the first of the baize doors.

'You're quite right, Bert,' Hilary said with a smile, 'the way to a man's heart is through his stomach.'

Ponting closed his eyes at the word 'stomach', and Hilary remarked at once: 'I hope you liked what came after the soup. They were quite English, you know. I thought it would be so unsuitable to import them from China. It was such an *English* luncheon. Ferney caught them in a cage.'

He closed the door softly, and walked down the passage, humming. What a very fortunate encounter. At his last words, Ponting had looked like a man drowning in an aquarium. And he did so hate being called Bert.

'Good evening, Rosemary.'

'Oh, good evening, sir.' Rosemary curtsied.

She was too pretty and good for that wet string bobbing outside the passage door. She was young, and alive on the earth; Ponting was old as Enoch Soames, and mostly dead under a fishy sea. He would have to destroy that idyll.

'Are you still in love?' Hilary asked, touching her eyelid with one long, white finger.

She wriggled back, blushed, tried to smile, and touched her own eyelid in wonder. Mr Byrd did that funny thing whenever he came near her, wherever she was, whoever was with him. 'I don't know what you mean,' she said. 'I'm not in love with anybody at all, sir.' Perhaps when he did that he was blessing her, like a bishop. But he asked her, when he touched her eyelid, things that she knew a bishop would never ask: 'How do you keep your stockings up?' 'Does Mavis wear bedsocks?' 'Would you like to blow your nose in my handkerchief?'

'Now, Rosemary,' he said, 'you know that I know everything that happens in the house. I have eyes that see everywhere, you know that, don't you, Rosemary?'

'Yes, sir.' She had seen his eyes in the clothes cupboard at night, on the stairs to bed, in the garden outside when she looked through her window before undressing. 'Oh yes, sir, but I'm not in love with anybody, I'm not, really.'

'There is a young man in this house,' Hilary said, 'who doesn't like women at all. Not at all. Do you understand? When he goes out with them he always takes his penknife with him.' He made a quick little movement with his fingers, suggesting something horrible. Then he left her abruptly and strode into the small passage between the two kitchens and mounted the servants' stairs.

Rosemary, alone, remembered Captain St John, 'a dagger through the throat' and the sharp-bladed knife. He was the man Mr Byrd had warned her against. The demon Captain, nasty as Crippen. Painted, too. Ugh! She thought with relief of her Mr Ponting with the sloppy eyes. Only three and a half hours to go.

Hilary stopped at a landing half-way up the circular tower staircase and knocked at a dark door.

'Come in,' said a voice.

'Come in through the keyhole,' said another.

'Under the door's quickest,' said the first voice.

Hilary opened the door and walked into the chauffeur's room. Mr Ferney and Quince, the Lacey coachman, were lying on the floor, flat on their backs, smoking cigarettes and counting aloud. The room was full of the sweet smell of hemp.

'Fifty-one, fifty-two, fifty-three,' said Mr Ferney slowly.

'Fifty-three,' Quince said. He was a white-haired, red-faced bucolic man of seventy or more, with mutton-chop whiskers, dressed in antique livery: a bad actor's impersonation of the family retainer.

'Fifty-three,' Mr Ferney said.

'Fifty-three,' said Quince.

They could not move beyond that number.

'Fifty-three, I'm Tom Thumb, I could sleep in the pocket of my coat.'

'I could run faster than Eclipse.'

'I could jump the Woolworth building.'

'Me too,' Quince said in a robust voice, 'I could run like a hare all over Dimbly.'

'Fifty-three.'

'The Lord and Ladies Lacey,' said Hilary at the door, 'are awaiting the coach.'

Quince tried to rise. 'Room too tiny,' he said. He managed at last to get on to his knees, and tried to shuffle to the door. 'I never been late, I never been late,' he said.

Mr Ferney reclined and puffed. The incredible, smoke-blue world caught him and juggled him quicker than a flying bullet.

'John William Quince, born eighteen-sixty-nine. Never been late all his life. Never kept a Lacey waiting. Fine old man.' Quince, on all fours now, had reached the door. 'Down the stairs in two ticks, sir.' He lurched forward, and downward, crying his name. Bump and 'Quince', bump and 'Quince'. Then a noise as of a barrel falling a long way into a cellar, and silence, and only Mr Ferney's monotonous, trancelike breathing and the curling of smoke in the airless room.

Hilary heard a roaring of engines in the stable yard, and began running down the stairs. Some of the victims must be escaping. He stepped over the hulk of Quince at the foot of the stairs. 'Fifty-three', ripely, and 'Quince is never late'. But Quince would be late that day.

As he ran into the yard he saw three cars. In the first sat pallid Jones and frail Berkeley. They were no loss.

Not seeing him, they drove off, talking, talking.

In the second car Atkins, bewildered but dignified. 'I looked for you everywhere, Mr Byrd, but could not find you to say goodbye. A very interesting time, indeed.' His feelings were outraged, but he never made a hasty decision. It sometimes took him months to make up his mind about the simplest things. Social matters required such a lot of thought. The real right thing. He felt it might be wrong to leave; on the other hand he really could not face the thought of prolonging his stay. There was a train at seven-thirty, and if Bartatt's old car would last for five miles he was determined to catch that train. His fabulously conventional baggage overflowed the back of the car; and round it peered Fergus O'Hara and Edmund Bell.

Snowden sat professional at the wheel of a little boy's dream-car, with Limpet as unwilling mechanic. He had sworn that he'd never face another journey in that car; but that was before he'd come to Dymmock. Snowden was quite imperturbable: life being true to a formula, one fitted everything into it, and out of the untidy portmanteau pulled one's poems. It would make a schoolgirlishly comic story for his three friends when he saw them next week in Brussels. Meantime, aloofness was the thing. The party had been quite out of period, but it could be fitted in somehow or other. Long live the formula. He sat woodenly as ever, peering through the goggles, heedless of Limpet's discomfort. Limpet had been ill.

Small fry, thought Hilary of these distinguished contemporaries.

'You're not going?' he said, solicitous.

Atkins repeated his speech. Perhaps they might meet in London and taste some cheese? he added. Bartatt let the clutch in abruptly, and the old car twitched forward before the Poet Laureate could reply.

The other car started too, Snowden stern at the wheel, Limpet slumped against him.

The dull great departed, Hilary stood for a few moments watching Bartatt's car bump down the drive. That Keystone Ford would, at any rate, shake a few poets up. He saw the car hop in a rut. That would rattle O'Hara to his watery marrow, and perhaps Edmund Bell would stop thinking of lichen. What would that uncomfortable journey do to Mr Atkins? Hilary wondered. Produce yet one more cautious revision of a compromise? another dead line for a verse to be recited on a canon's birthday? another jingle for his latest dog-book? As the car skidded round the corner on two wheels, Hilary remembered with pleasure the opening lines of a new light poem he had found in Atkins's overcoat pocket while examining the guests' cloakroom before lunch:

> *Bubble and Bow-wow and Viscount Squeak,*
> *The chow, the bullpup, and the peke,*
> *Bound all day on a barkable lark*
> *Towsering round the peagreen park.*

If only Bartatt would drive the poets into a ditch. He was certainly very unsteady, and the commission he had nagged and beaten from Philip Lacey to sculpt an enormous lead figure of that small man might make him even more forgetful.

Snowden's monster would be nearly at the station by now. Limpet would have been ill again. He did not care what happened to Snowden so long as the journey was unsuccessful and resulted in a poem.

> *Continue, blond albino, in your catapulting sportscar,*
> *Leaping among pylons in your new MG,*
> *Two birdwatchers and a clean-limbed guardsman*
> *Are awaiting your arrival with a cup of milky tea,*

he extemporized idly as he walked back through the dining hall and out into the main courtyard.

The fair was nearly ready. Some Mr Hartleys were setting their midget house in order, and the one who had been bitten by the pike – he was easy to recognize because of his comparative smallness – was practising shadow-boxing, and punching himself quite hard. At the sight of Hilary, he stopped at once and raised a cry. 'Benjamin, Willie, Lennox, Christian, Arnold, here's Lord Tennyson who made me bathe with the sharks.'

The front of the midget house had not yet been closed, and out of the four rooms, from bed and cupboard and bath, five Mr Hartleys rushed to his aid, carrying crockery, rolling pins, and little pokers.

'Good evening,' Hilary said. 'Welcome again to Locksley Hall.'

'Who took Constant upstairs in a pram?'

'Who gave Constant smelly stuff?'

'Constant's got six stitches.'

The Mr Hartleys shook their weapons, and danced with anger all about their house. One Mr Hartley cried, from a safe distance, 'His Lordship's a bully,' and another, at the top of the stairs, flourished a tiny razor.

'Have any of you,' Hilary asked, 'seen anything of a Great Dane? I'm afraid he broke loose from his kennel. He's such a surly fellow, and I forgot to feed him this morning.'

The Mr Hartleys stopped still. Constant, the smallest, climbed upstairs into the bedroom and got into bed quite slowly, drawing the sheets over his head.

'Nelson likes meat,' Hilary said, 'red meat, of course. And bones. If you see him about, just throw him something, will you?'

He walked off, through a cluster of tents and stalls, to the caravans at the end of the courtyard. 'Oh, Mr Daniel,' he called out before a caravan painted over with red lions, 'can I come up?' He did not wait for an answer, but mounted the steps and entered the smoky living room, to find Cornelius and the lion-tamer talking Swedish. From their gestures, and from the smacking noises they made with their lips whenever one particular word was spoken, Hilary gathered immediately the subject of their conversation.

'I'm sorry to interrupt you, but I wanted to know if all the arrangements were in order for tonight,' he said.

Daniel, a fat, smiling man clad already in his lion-skin, with a stock-whip across his bare knees, winked and replied: 'Everything ready to scratch. Especially Big Johnny.'

'Are you sure the cage is properly locked?'

Daniel winked again. 'All in order. Johnny in a rage tonight. Purposely I did not tickle him goodbye when I leave him.'

'Good. I hope you'll enjoy the show, Cornelius.'

'We talking dames,' said Cornelius politely, 'scram, please.'

As Hilary went out, he heard that one word repeated loudly several times. They were warming up to their subject again.

And now, he said to himself, stepping over tent-ropes, kicking the sawdust, peering quickly into the dark dens of snake-charmer, fortune-teller, lightning calculator, strong man, and tattooed lady, now for my last inspection of the upper floors, of the bedrooms and bathrooms and burrows, the comic intimacies and intrigues, the queer people alone working at their damnation, the drunks at their sad games. He dramatized the petty follies of his guests into infernal scenes as he went into the house and made his way upstairs.

The first bedroom was empty. In the second Robin Shelley lay asleep on the bed: it would take more than the touch of his finger on her eyelid to waken her now.

Two men were speaking in the third bedroom, their voices loud with recrimination. He paused and listened through the door. Basil Minto was cataloguing again.

'Exactly what I've always said: the man's a mere *practical joker*. A tasteless Horace Cole, absolutely fuddled with the nineties and the tens and the twenties and the rest of the between-war escape.'

'*Queerly true.*'

Hilary could imagine the Japanese death-mask tilted in agreement over Bull Dudley's tattered tie.

'Of course, one knew all that before: the introvert's exhibitionism, the whole narcissistic rigmarole. It's the *blatancy* of the thing that's so astonishing.'

'Very odd.'

'And why do it at all? It's just an Aunt Sally show. The dummies fall over, and there's an end of it. Not the *subtlest* performance, either. Not enough friction to make it satisfying.'

'Curious.'

'It isn't as though one *minded*, even. What's the motive? Jealousy, probably. I knew he was furious that I never asked him for anything for *Sunrise*. But then one *is* more or less civilized.'

'*Strange.*'

'Perhaps he feels that life is false to formula after all. Wyndham told Christopher that Hilary wrote to Adrian from Fez that pure individualism wasn't sufficiently justified. It was after he'd been gun-running for Franco. *All right.* But I'd have thought he was just mature enough not to go in for these private-school sulks. He's probably become impotent. They *say* . . .'

Feet drowned the complaining whinny. Pat Barrington came flying down the corridor, if not for her virtue, for her life. Her pursuer was Christopher Garvin, an altered

Christopher, a berserk giant with bloodshot blue eyes, who shouted in pursuit.

'He must have eaten of some strange red herb,' Hilary quoted as he moved on in the direction from which they had come. Mrs Barrington in retreat twice in the same day! A pretty paradox.

Through an open bathroom door he saw a Laocöon-like group swaying and cursing.

'Tak' his legs, mon.'

'No, no! Over his head.'

'My *ears*! Mind my ears!'

Eric Wetley had chosen his companions badly. Gorman and McManus were not the ideal couple to help him out of his indiarubber suit.

'The hairs!'

'Never mind the hairs. Keep your daft legs still.'

'Let's cut him out.'

'Bide a minute. I've a clasp-knife here . . .'

'Keep still.'

A shriller scream than before. Eric Wetley would regret the loss of that indiarubber suit; and perhaps the loss of more besides.

Hilary left him to his fate, and knocked at the next bedroom door.

Julian Greensleaves rose to meet him.

'Really excellent, Julian. I congratulate you.'

Julian Greensleaves sat down again at the mirror. Yes: it was a pretty good make-up. The arched nose, the very black hair above the upcurving eyebrows, the deep lines from nostrils to sardonic mouth.

'It'll do, I think.'

'It's superb.'

'Adequate. It's not absolutely right, but it'll pass to-night.'

'I'll send Porson up with something cold, and a bottle of claret. I may join you later.'

Greensleeves' masquerade would be of great help to the confusion he had planned for the night. Two Laureates appearing at dark corners; one running suddenly out of a tent of freaks, the other following him a second later out of the same tent to confront the spectators and fill them with doubt; one sitting in a chair near Gordon in the library, and the other walking in; both creeping and hunting among the shadows in the turbulent courtyard: what Minto had said was true, these were the unpleasant practical jokes of a dated man out of love, but he would not part with them. There was nothing to take their place but the terrible monotony of the working intellect, the groans and self-whippings, the false flashes and sterile wastes of exhibitionist creation, the slow death of 'being together', the dungeons of being alone.

Round a corner at the far end of the corridor, two women, one in underclothes, the other Yvonne Bacon, scampered, squealing. From a deep doorway Hilary watched them.

The woman in underclothes was Prudence Whittier, that elegant American who liked her poets to be men. As Owen Tudor rushed the corner after them Prudence giggled to Yvonne who was pretending to escape, 'He certainly isn't wrapped in cellophane, is he? Look at that lovelight, Yvonne. Oh, be your age, poet.' She pushed him away with no conviction.

'You're my nymphs, *my* nymphs,' Tudor shouted, 'Phyllida! Amaryllis.' He tried to embrace them both. 'You're *my* goddesses,' he gloated, 'you and you and you and *you*.' At the last shout he threw himself upon Yvonne Bacon and bore her to the ground.

'*Such* fun,' Yvonne said in a muffled voice. It was her titter of anticipation as he stooped above her, crying,

'Amaryllis, Amaryllis,' that brought him to his senses. He rose to his feet and staggered against the wall. He ran his hands through his wild hair. He hiccuped once.

'Say, what's come over you? Why aren't you doing something? Don't tell me the party's over. You've got hiccups,' Prudence said.

Yvonne lay still. She had, anyway, never expected it to happen.

Tudor closed his eyes, opened them, looked hard at the two women, and closed them again.

'You'd better come along with us and drink out of a glass the wrong way round. I must say you're a dim bulb all of a sudden. Come on, Yvonne. Romeo's got a bellyache.'

The women walked down the corridor, one haughtily, one unsteadily, and Tudor followed them. As he passed the bedroom door, Hilary heard him mutter in amazement: 'Yvonne! Yvonne Bacon! Iessi Crist!' And his voice grew fainter: 'Nymphs! Oh dear! TT now. Ever and ever amen. Yvonne Bacon! What *have* I done?'

Hilary emerged from hiding.

He walked up to his baby Bluebeard's room. Rather to his surprise, he heard voices in there. Like a pigeon, Hamish Corbie had winged home. With him, Ostler; and shrewd Mallow, sensing a link with his period. Sadie Lowenstein and Mona Boylan were in the window-seat.

'Hail, neophyte,' said the Master in a reedy voice, 'just dipping into your incunabula.'

'Is that what you call it? It looks like plain dirt to me.'

'Miss Boylan is perhaps not altogether familiar with esoteric phenomena.'

'You flatter me, Ostler. I like Mona's description of my little collection very much.'

'You certainly have been around. Oh boy!' said Sadie.

'The way to the truth is hard. He who would attain the ultimate vision must be prepared to suffer. He who would be immune from desire must experience all desires.'

'Who wants to be immune from desire, anyway?'

'Experiences await him who can endure, such as may not be dreamt of. Do you mind if I smoke a cigar?'

Hilary looked at the gross, decaying figure of the sage, at the two fever-eyed women, at the pathetically dignified Ostler. Mallow, with an occasional whistle, was looking through a portfolio of drawings.

He went down the twisting stair. Time to see the villagers assembled at the long trestle tables in the courtyard; time to see that the booths and sideshows were prepared; time to break one's fast and have a whisky-and-soda. He reached the hall. It was very still in the June evening. The faint bustle, outside, of the men putting the finishing touches to the fairground was the only sound. The villagers would be arriving any minute now. He rang the bell.

Porson dragged his flat feet over the marble. 'I was looking for you, sir, all over the house.'

'What's wrong?'

'I was going down to the wine-cellar, sir, when I heard something.'

'What sort of something?'

'Horrible, sir. Like what Sir Austin used to say *he* heard. Clanking and groaning and gnashing. Regular tribulation. You've raised them up, sir.'

'Raised what up, Porson?'

'The ghosts of Dymmock, sir. Mad Giles and Headless Humphrey and the Toad in the Wall.'

'Get me a torch and a strong stick.'

Porson went quaking away, and Hilary descended the cellar stairs. The cellars were built in the original Norman substructure, and elaborately heated, but beyond them stretched great cavernous silences, medieval storerooms and dungeons and a vaulted torture-chamber.

'Don't you want your torch and stick, sir?' Porson called from above.

'Shall I send for Ferney, sir?'

'You can if you *like*, Porson.'

He went on down the stairs.

There was indeed a strange noise. Clanking and groaning, certainly, if not gnashing. He went through the darkness to the torture-chamber and pushed open the iron-studded door. Two candles lit up a curious scene. Oliver Fry dangled upside down from the ceiling, casting alarming shadows. Looking like a suppressed page of Carlyle's *French Revolution*, Magda Crawshay turned at a rusty winch, in spite of his groans, and with each turn his fettered limbs were stretched another fraction.

'It's enough, I tell you.'

'Nonsense. Have the *courage* of your *convictions*. If you want to understand Sade you must be prepared to *suffer*.'

'I am, I am prepared, but let me down.'

'All right. But then you must try the rack.'

'Anything! Only my head's spinning.'

'Your tail'll be spinning when we've racked you. Hullo, Byrd, nice Byrd.'

She let go of the winch, and Fry rattled and jangled to the floor.

'My head!'

'Never mind about your head. You think of the principle of the thing.'

Fry looked beyond the reach of principle, but Breton had told him to have faith, and Dali had made him a pair of masochistic delirium pyjamas, and his garden was full of Arps. They helped him out of his fetters, and he moved wearily to the great rack.

'Take your clothes off.'

'What for?'

'You can't be racked in a lounge suit.'

Hilary excused himself, pleading hostly duties. Looking back from the door he saw a pale figure stretched out in resignation.

Magda Crawshay spat on her hands.

Upstairs, Hilary Byrd walked out into the evening.

CHAPTER SEVEN

NIGHT BIRDS

THE police would probably not be there for an hour at least, and nobody in the courtyard gave them a thought. It was ten o'clock. A panatrope sounded over the crack of rifles, the smashing of crockery, the complaining of beasts – hyenas, a mandrill, some performing dogs, and Big Johnny the lion. The village maidens shrilled on slide or behind tent. The flares were beginning to show more brilliantly against the now dark-blue summer sky. The whole scene was lively yet mysterious, at once bright and menacing.

'Breughel,' said Agard.

'It's a Walpurgisnacht.'

'No, it isn't a bit. It's gay. You're too complicated.'

'My God, Tom, is *that* gay?'

Agard followed Tudor's finger.

'Uncomplicated, anyway.'

'I don't agree at all,' Tudor bawled. 'How could it be, shut in these walls? It's not a midsummer fair, it's a mid-night mass.'

'Have it your own way. I feel benign tonight.'

'It's entirely a question of mood, what you see. You've been pigging yourself on music and claret, while I've been depriving myself, very stupidly, of . . .'

'It wasn't stupid, it was very wise. And the sleep has done you good.'

'Never mind. Let it be Walpurgisnacht, but I won't be answerable for the consequences. This is a warning! There's blood in the sky. And by that token there is cognac in my flask. Tom, I forgive you.'

125

'Get up, and stop slavering. Do you think that slide would hold me?'

'No. Think what might happen at the bottom.'

Tudor pointed to the struggling mass of sliders at the foot of the shaft. Some of the London young ladies were making the most of themselves, and the vicar's sleeve was torn right across by Mrs Hubble's tugging.

'Let's start off with a peep at the future. Then we can make our plans for the evening. There's Corbie's tent.'

Outside the sign of the Great Raven, Tudor tossed a coin that he had borrowed from Prudence Whittier on the pretence of having to lend it to a friend in need, and called, 'Heads I go in first, Tom, tails you go in second.' He did not expect the subterfuge to work, though it was always worth trying.

Tom Agard saw the half-crown come down tails. 'I go in first, then,' he said.

'No, second,' Tudor said, without hope.

Agard patted him kindly on the shoulder. 'You can listen at the flap,' he said. He walked into the tent.

'I don't want to listen at the flap,' Tudor said aloud to himself. 'Who wants to hear the Great Raven anyway? It's only old Dirty dressed up like a woman. Charlatan.' He pressed his ear to the canvas.

'One shilling down,' said the voice of the Great Raven from within. 'Two and six for very private information.' The voice sank to a whisper. 'Women. Sex. What the future holds for your . . .' Tudor could not catch the word. 'Very secret. Horrible.' Tudor fingered the half-crown.

It was hard to hear everything for the noise of the fair around him: Sousa on the panatrope, the screaming and laughter, the explosions of the first fireworks, 'Seven for sixpence, every ball a winner,' 'Try your luck, lady,' 'I'm not a lady, I'm Hubert,' 'There she goes,' 'What'll you have, sir, the Felix or the flower vase?' 'I'll have a small Haig.' But he could make out much of what the Great Raven said.

The high voice droned from the tent: 'I see a stretch of water, turquoise and indigo, and a boat full of musicians. Shem Iram Agah! There is a tall flautist under Virgo, beware of her after sundown. The boat is rocking, the waves are full of instruments. You have been drowned,' the voice concluded mildly.

'He only had a shilling's worth,' Tudor said to the dark.

Agard was not satisfied, either. 'What's the name of the flautist?'

'I see the letter B. The rest is clouded. There is doom for you in her name.'

'Nice doom?'

'B and a cloud. The crystal is darkening. Question me quickly.'

'Is it Betty?'

'Nay.'

'Beatrice, Bunnie, Babette? Let it be Beatrice, Great Raven. I met her in Paris. I played Rameau with her.'

'I bet,' said the Great Raven. 'Time's up. The future is burning out. I cannot see. The clouds are gathering. I dare not look. Mind the rope. Next, please.'

As Agard came out of the tent, he said to Tudor, 'Did you listen?'

'No, not a word.'

'He said Beatrice Hautbois was my doom.'

Tudor strutted in. Poor old Tom. You couldn't expect Beatrice Hautbois for a shilling.

'Two and a tanner,' Agard heard him whisper. 'I don't want the ordinary stuff. I want the very private. . . . I'm not in a hurry. . . .'

'What are you up to? Eavesdropping? Come and smash

E*   127

some plates.' Gordon appeared at Agard's elbow, carrying a celluloid doll. 'Hoopla,' he explained. 'Lady Lucretia won everything else. Damned good shot.'

He took Agard's arm, and they gavotted through the tent-ropes.

'Lady Lucretia's a very charming person, don't you think, Agard?'

'All right if you like freaks. Let's go in here and see some professional ones.'

'No, but seriously . . .'

'Seriously charming, yes. Have you got two sixpences?'

They were alone in the tent. The ragged curtain twitched, but nobody entered. They waited.

'*She* doesn't fit in with Byrd and all that sort of thing.'

'I'm not so sure that she doesn't; but don't talk too loudly.'

'What on earth do you mean? You don't mean to imply that they ever . . . ?'

'I don't imply anything, my dear Gordon.'

'Because if you did, I'd punch your head for you.'

'Do stop talking. Here she is.'

The curtain parted and the bearded lady came in. A small man in barker's evening dress came in behind her, and began telling the lady's story in a flat Arkansas voice. She was thirty-three and had two children by her third husband. You could pull the beard if you liked. Apart from that, normal in every respect, with a figure famous sculptors had declared to be perfection. The little man's eyes wandered dully as he spoke. The bearded lady discreetly revealed her charms.

Gordon was entranced, Lady Lucretia momentarily forgotten, but Agard turned as Hilary Byrd entered. A second's pause, and Hilary had left the tent as abruptly as he'd come in, leaving Agard staring after him. Frowning, the barker muttered something and went behind the curtain.

Agard, curious, followed Byrd. He heard Gordon's 'I say, are you ever in London? Don't know if you'd ever care to dine with me some evening.' Outside, Byrd had disappeared. Cursing loudly, Agard stumbled over the tent-ropes, then fell on his back and saw stars. Fireworks, too. Why not stay where he was? Let bearded ladies and Byrds and ladybirds go hang. *Feux d'artifice*: Debussy, Stravinsky . . .

Inside the Great Raven's tent the future grew horrible indeed. Corbie, clothed in an elaborate black Victorian evening gown, ear-ringed and braceleted, his jowls rouged, his thick mouth painted, wearing a high red wig and a bonnet with a veil, sat on a stool behind a table and read, from the crystal, the news of imminent depravity. On the floor behind him a bottle poked out of a fish frail. An acetylene lamp hung over the table, casting shadows on their faces, making the corners alive. Two eyes watched Tudor from under the table. He hoped they belonged to a cat.

'I see a plain thick with bushes. The bushes are rippling. A hand comes out with a stocking in it. A bare leg kicks under the bush. Wait, I can see more. A limb protrudes . . .'

'Are those cat's eyes, please?'

'What eyes? Do you want to know what's in the crystal or not?'

'Oh yes, of course, but there's something looking at me.'

'A limb protrudes, covered in fur.'

Tudor began to wish he had not consulted the future. It would be safer breaking plates or teasing the midgets. There was a snake-dancer round the corner who had been conducted out of Brighton by the police. He heard the rockets shooting.

'I must be going now, Corbie.'

'Great Raven.'

'Great Raven. I've got to see the snake-dancer. She's only twenty and Hilary told me . . .'

'Their fangs have been removed.'

'That's good. That's a pity, I mean. There won't be any deaths tonight.'

Tudor tried to laugh. The feeble dry noise made him shiver. The cat under the table closed one eye. If it was not a cat, one light went out. He looked away, and saw through the open flaps of the tent a figure twelve feet high stalking in the summer moonlight. 'There's a man on stilts out there,' he said. Hilary had not mentioned him.

'For another shilling I can see death.'

'I haven't any money with me.'

'Sixpence.'

'I can give you some cigarettes.'

Great Raven nodded. The wig danced like a bonfire.

'Marijuana,' he said, as he lit one of the cigarettes.

'I took them from a box at lunch. Do they make you . . .' Tudor hesitated, remembering the incident in the corridor . . . 'full of fun? I mean, do they make you want to do things?' He blushed in the darkness, and said in a sly voice: 'Larks.'

'Sleep. Sleep and dream. Nepenthe, necropolis, time and space twined in one serpent. The Sphinx is woven in smoke.'

'Well, it's been nice . . .'

'I see death over Dymmock.' The bracelets jingled, the wig slipped, one hairy hand described a circle under the hanging lamp. 'The mark of the beast.' Said Corbie, 'It runs over the crystal like a plague. Who lieth dead in a knot of dwarfs? I cannot see the name.'

'It doesn't start with a T, I suppose?' Tudor asked. Under the table the second light went out. Perhaps the cat was asleep.

'I can see no more, the crystal is darkening.'

'Or an O?'

'I see no more. The cloud has dropped.' The hand blessed the air. 'Next, please.'

Tudor, hurrying out, passed Albert Ponting at the entrance to the tent. He paused long enough to hear Ponting's nervous voice and the whispered answer:

'I've got a friend who's going to meet another friend at eleven o'clock tonight and I wanted to know if you could tell me what was going to happen so that I could tell my friend.'

'Two and six. Sit down. The crystal is glowing. I see a mouth full of teeth, and a hank of hair.'

Tudor ran in the direction of the tent of the snake-dancer. Time after time a bell rang near by out of the flared night. People were breaking china.

'Oh, you bloody little man, look where you're going.'

'Sorry, Tom.'

'It's you, is it? What was it like in the Great Raven's nasty nest?'

'Nasty. A winking cat, a smell of garlic, and death prophesied in the dark.'

'All for a *shilling*?'

'No. Half a crown. Dirty rate. Did you break that flask when you fell, you whale?'

'Let us arise and see.'

'Boozing again?' said a languid little voice.

'Hello, Roger. Afraid the flask's empty.'

'There's a case of champagne in my car.'

'How nice. Let's go there. But why, exactly?'

'You never know when you're not going to be stranded. I don't like to be at a loss in the country. Besides, somebody might be ill.'

'Never mind his reasons,' said Tudor, 'where's the car?'

As they passed the midget house they saw Dudley and Minto, mutually informative.

'Solly Zuckerman says somewhere that the great apes are infinitely more intelligent.'

'Probably queerly true. The Dalai Lama showed me the Chinese translation. It was after one of my Housman readings. But more intelligent than what?'

'Oh, all of us. Especially this sort, I meant.'

'I know Mr Zuckerman,' cried Constant Hartley. 'He's got much better manners than you.'

'Yes,' said Benjamin Hartley, darkly. 'Our time will come! We'll strike one day, and then you'll know what's what.'

'They haven't paid to talk to us,' shouted Lennox Hartley, flinging down a miniature *Fanny Hill*.

'Or about us.'

'Very rude.'

'Unkind and inconsiderate.'

'Stupid, too.'

'Really,' Agard said as they walked on, 'those undersized fellows make one feel quite ashamed.'

They reached the yard, and Roger picked out his Duisenberg, massive against the meaner metal, powerful in the moon. He was about to fumble in the back of the car when voices came from the front seat, oblivious of him, or Agard, or Tudor, or any other man.

'Darling, I thought you were a girl.'

'I always knew you were. Right from the start.'

'You're so clever, aren't you, darling?'

'I'm so really clever that I think I know best about that little silver box.'

'It isn't as easy as you think. Once you start. I think I might go mad and do something quite awful if I stopped.'

'Isn't it worth the risk? Anything is, if you hate it

enough. Evil things need destroying. I know who started you on this: I'll attend to him later. Get rid of the stuff first – that's your job.'

A small bright object curved out of the car and fell with a splinter of glass.

'O Lord, I've broken somebody's windscreen.'

'You've broken a hell of a lot more than that, sweet Robin.'

'I think I can bear it. The extraordinary thing is that your name should be Captain St John. *Captain St John.* You must have some deeply secret other name. O darling darling Captain St John.'

Holding their fingers to their lips and hushing one another fiercely, the three friends walked away from the car. Tudor and Rashleigh, two short, light men, made a noise on the cobbles like ponies trotting; Agard padded soft as a cat.

'Well, well,' Tudor said, 'that was a very funny thing to hear. And no champagne either.'

'What do you mean, funny?' Agard said. 'Is it funny to hear a man and a woman saying that they're in love? Not everybody is a twilit pederast, even in Dymmock. You're a muckraker and a dirt-box if you think that a decent sexual relationship is just another laugh for your loathsome Cardiff friends. You're the sort of man who thinks that the birth of babies is an obscene custard-pie act. You'd stick pins through rubber goods. You'd read Housman to a twelve-year-old schoolgirl.'

'I have,' Tudor said.

'Liar.'

'Thief.'

'Blackmailer.'

'Bad poet.'

'I think the whole scene was perfectly obvious from the start,' Rashleigh began. Nothing surprised him. He made vague gestures indicating, to his imagination, that the night itself was a bare commonplace and that the activities of the people in it were all dull and inevitably unsatisfactory. The gestures might have been those of a man describing a washing machine, or pointing out the stars.

'So it's perfectly obvious, is it, old riddle of the Kremlin?'

'You knew all about it beforehand, I suppose? You never thought St John was a queer boy, oh no.'

Agard and Tudor turned on Rashleigh together.

'Uncle Joe's pocket knowall.'

'Unshockable Rashleigh, the Clerkenwell medium.'

'He's got a Red Bird who tells him everything.'

'I only said that I thought . . .'

' – There was some champagne in that great vulgar car of yours. I'm dry as a kipper.'

'So am I.'

'Shh! There's Hilary.' Tudor pointed to a figure in the shadow of a caravan.

'What's he doing?'

'He's just standing. Can't a man just stand any more?'

'Hello, Hilary.'

'Hello, girls. Out on the spree?'

They left him standing bareheaded and lone under the caravan window.

'I loathe that affectation of ancient slang,' said Agard.

'Can't think what he's doing there,' Roger said.

'Thought you knew everything,' Tudor muttered.

As they passed an unlit caravan just before the cluster of tents, Hilary Byrd trod softly down the steps and paused in front of them.

'God Almighty,' said Tudor. He pinched Agard on the arm. 'Am I dreaming?'

'The proper thing to do if you think you're dreaming,' Agard said, 'is to pinch yourself.'

'It hurts *me*.'

'Hello, Hilary, you get around a lot.' Roger waved his hand.

'Where have you four been?' asked Hilary. 'I haven't seen you all night.' He went up the caravan steps again and closed the door.

'Perhaps we had better forget that,' Agard said. 'I don't want to hear another word about Hilary. He must have run round behind the caravans.'

'But he didn't have time.'

'And he had a hat on this time.'

'There's only three of us, anyway.' Tudor was doubtful. He kept very close to his friends.

'It's best not to worry at all. I'll take you both on at the rifle range.'

Agard led the way. Tudor and Rashleigh muttered behind him.

'Tom and you and me, that's one two three.'

'He had a kind of bowler on.'

'Tom, Roger, Tudor . . .'

'Come on, don't argue. Look, Oliver Fry's over there. He's banging away at that strength machine like a giant.'

Before a dumb crowd of anarchists and villagers, Fry raised the heavy hammer and brought it down upon the anvil. The bell of Barney's Try Your Strength Machine rang for the twentieth time that night. He wiped his forehead on a hand-painted handkerchief, paid his threepence to a bewildered man who stood near by, and raised the hammer again.

'You don't want to hit it again, mister,' Barney pleaded, turning to the crowd for sympathy. 'He's won all the gold-fish and a Minnie Mouse and a Jollicum and a pair of bicycle clips and a cigarette case. He doesn't want to hear the bell any more, does he, ladies and gentlemen?'

Fry brought the hammer down, the bell rang, a small leather bear was produced from a sack, and he paid another threepence.

'He's at it again,' Barney said. 'Bang, boom, bang, boom, all the night it's bang, boom. Haven't you got a home to go to, mister?'

The bell rang.

'Now, look, I'll give you a signed certificate to say you can bang my bell *any* time you like. I'll put it down in black-and-white that you're the strongest chap I've ever seen. I'll give you a Shirley Temple Doll and a free pass to the bearded lady. I'll give you a Donald Duck and a large Players'. I can't say fairer than that. Only stop ringing that bell.'

The bell rang. O'Brien, Mahaffy, McManus and Gorman watched the hammer rise again with envy and bewilderment.

'I'll make it two Donald Ducks. And another Jollicum. You can have Mrs Barney.'

The bell rang.

'Twice. Three times. Mrs Barney used to be on the trapeze.'

Agard, Tudor, and Rashleigh moved on among the bodies and faces. Sir Frank Knight, mottled and nettled, was flung up like a bottle in the backwash. Christopher Garvin, stringy as an emu, with Pat Barrington, humbled, under his wing.

Outside the tent of the Great Chronos, Lightning Calculator, 'The Most Amazing Mathematician in the World', the wizard stood and waited.

'I've seen that man before,' said Agard. 'Now, where?' Then he remembered the sad-eyed describer of the bearded lady's virtues. 'So *he's* the father of the "two perfectly normal children". Well, well, well!'

Great Chronos went inside his tent, having a sufficient audience.

'Time's an enemy,' said Tudor. 'Let's keep going.'

At the next booth the rifles were red-hot. Mona Boylan was letting off from both hips with pioneer precision, knocking down celluloid balls and strings of animals. Her father's booth on Coney Island would have been proud of her. More astonishing, at her side the Ladies Crystal and Lucretia were no less deadly, if more stately. Their father had once slaughtered six hundred birds at one stand. King Edward had been their sponsor.

'I shouldn't like to annoy any of those three.'

'They look murderous enough already.'

'What images are they slaughtering, do you suppose?'

'Critics and gossips, and the normal and the insulting.'

'Hilary Byrd.'

A crash followed by a triumphant shout turned their heads to the cock-shy next to the rifle-range. Magda Crawshay had done it again. Having first demolished the targets, she had turned to the prizes.

Now nothing remained but the terrified proprietor himself, whose beseeching face bobbed up every so often from behind the shattered stand, his expostulations severed each time by a whizz and a thud as the remaining wooden balls were discharged past his head into the canvas backing.

'Stand up and take it, you wretched rat.'

'Please, madam, I . . .'

'What are you ducking for, you old monster?'

'My china!'

'Never saw such a lily-livered dwarf!'

'A fine sight,' said Agard. 'I told you I smelt blood. Magda's a man-eater.'

'Let's move on while she still has her sense of direction. I'm hungry.'

'And I'm thirsty.'

'Never knew you when you weren't.'

'One gets thirsty,' Roger said thoughtfully.

They looked at him.

'The phenomenon.'

'The great thinker.'

Magda turned her attention to the stacked prizes in the hoop-la competition. Once again the crash of china, and the smash of glass.

Tudor was growing impatient of destruction. 'Anyone can break a plate,' he said, 'I broke a mirror this morning.' Suddenly he thought of two luminous eyes under a table. 'Bad luck,' he said aloud to himself, 'oh, bad, bad luck.' The staring black cat, the prophecy of death in Dymmock, the furry limb in the crystal, the aberration in the corridor, the twelve-foot moonlight walker, and Hilary seen all over the place like a man in a circle of mirrors: all the separate mysteries of the night now shuddered into one. 'Have you seen the stiltwalker?' he asked.

'There isn't a stiltwalker,' Agard said.

Tudor raised his head to the moon, and howled like a dog. The rockets hissed him; the naphtha jets bubbled one awful word around him; the music loudened to a storm and chased him down sawdust-sprinkled aisles between tents full of abominations. 'I'm in at the *death*,' a woman with a bow and arrow shouted to a friend who could not be seen. He tripped over a couple on the ground. 'I could *kill* you,' one writhing figure said to the other. He heard, as he ran, Tom Agard shout behind him: 'Where's that *madman* running? After him, Roger.' '*Slash* 'em on the top to win,' a stall-keeper cried. A firework burst above him like a dragon bombed, all tails and forks and tongues. '*Shoot* for the whites of their eyes.' Barney's bell rang loud above the rising music. 'Walk up, walk up, to see the *Freaks*.' Agard stamped behind him. 'Walk up, walk up. The tattooed *devil* from the Congo. The Beaked Woman.' Tudor raced towards the house. He would shelter in the kitchen among the safe and comfortable pots and pans. He would block his ears and shut his eyes fast and think of honey and Sunday mornings in the suburbs and cats asleep on the hearth. Cats! A winking firework with a long tail sped up the sky, and two great hands clutched him around the shoulders.

'Woa there, Owen,' Agard said. 'Come on, Roger, get him by the legs.'

They brought Tudor to the ground, and straddled over him.

'It's best to sit on his chest,' Roger said. His cigarette glowed like a cat's eye.

'Don't let Tom sit on me,' shouted Tudor, trying to rise.

'Push him down.'

'Let's make a straitjacket. A chap I used to know could make a straitjacket out of an ordinary woman's corset and some wire. You just have to bind the . . .'

'I was only going to the house to find a bottle.'

'Why did you howl, then?'

'I was thirsty.'

'You don't howl if you're thirsty.'

'I do.'

'You bayed to the moon. Everybody heard you. They said, "There's Owen Tudor baying to the moon," didn't they, Roger?'

A man rose out of the darkness.

'Anyone dead?' Hilary Byrd asked in a polite voice, bending down to stare at Tudor.

'Owen's pretending he's a dog, aren't you, Owen?'

'I was only looking for a bottle.'

'There's an unopened case in the lower kitchen,' Hilary

said. 'And there's a kennel outside the door. Are you enjoying the fair?' He bowed, and walked swiftly back to the tents.

'We can chain Tudor up and give him a bottle in the kennel,' Agard said. He helped Tudor to his feet. 'You take one arm, Roger.' Tudor was frogmarched along, struggling and complaining.

As they went up the kitchen steps, they heard voices speaking from the shelter of the door. A man, who had been hidden in the shadows, brushed by them and ran down the steps and across the courtyard.

'Did you see who that was?' Tudor whispered.

Agard and Roger released their hold on him.

'It looked like Hilary,' Roger said. He dropped his cigarette.

'It was Hilary.' Agard swore softly. He crept towards the door.

'Did you hear anything, Rosemary?' a voice asked.

'I thought I heard somebody whispering. It must have been the wind. Or Mr Byrd looking for things in the dark. I've seen him at all sorts of funny hours, prowling round the house. Albert, do you think he could have seen us when we . . . when we . . . Oh, I'm sure I saw his eyes. I saw him looking at me from the linen cupboard once.'

Tudor, behind a hedge, moaned and put his handkerchief in his mouth.

'There, what's that? That wasn't the wind.'

'I'll take care of you, Rosemary. Don't let go of me. Lots of things make noises in the night, it's nothing to be frightened about. Crickets and frogs and owls and . . .'

'That wasn't an owl. Owls go tu-wit tu-woo. Frogs go grrrk. And I know what crickets sound like, they live under my bedroom window.'

'Where is your bedroom?'

'Oh, you mustn't say that. Ask no questions and you'll hear no lies. It's at the very top of the servants' stairs, on the right.'

'Can I move my arm, Rosemary? I've got pins and needles.'

'Move it here. No, not there, silly. And, no, not there either. There!'

There was a long pause. Agard tried to creep back to the courtyard, but he stumbled against a bush.

'I heard something moving.'

'*You're* frightened now. I don't care how many ghosts there are, they can do anything they like. There's one now, with his head under his arm. Whoo! Whoo!' Then the voice grew soft: 'I was only joking.'

In the longer silence that followed, Agard removed himself from the bush and beckoned to his friends. Tudor did not want to go. They drove him forward, pressing their knuckles into his back. He did not dare cry out.

'Are you frightened now?' Rosemary asked.

'You mustn't move away from me,' said Albert Ponting. 'I wouldn't know what to do. I've never liked anybody else.'

'You can come and have tea with my mother on Sunday.'

'I don't want your mother. I want you, Rosemary. Oh, Rosemary . . .'

For the second time that night, three abashed and thirsty men tiptoed under the moon, each making unnecessarily elaborate gestures to secure the silence of the other two.

'It's a conspiracy, all this love, to keep us from our liquor.'

'You're a great cask of slush,' Tudor was angry.

'Let's go and have another try at my car.'

They went again into the courtyard and the fair, Agard whistling through his nose, the other two leaning inwards like those trained elephants which are brought in to control the newly captured furious bull.

A fresh noise, cored in the clamour, spiralled up with the rockets.

'What's Magda doing now?'

'Putting a half-Nelson on the bearded lady?'

The edges of the crowd frayed. Dark figures began running aimlessly, madly, to the panatrope's Petrouchka. The voices went up several tones, and they cried in the rhythm of fright: 'The lion! Lion! The lion's escaped!'

'Lions don't escape,' said Agard. Then he heard the coughing roar, and did not repeat himself.

Everyone was running. It was like a forest fire. Magda Crawshay, Eric Wetley under one arm and William Dudley under the other, trotted to the lily pond and dropped them in. The slide began to fill with figures crawling upwards with nightmare slowness. Basil Minto, too frightened to get up, screamed and screamed where he had fallen. Roger lit a long cigar, while Agard and Tudor ran swifter than any to the Duisenberg. It was empty. They did not hurry. Several minutes passed before they rejoined Roger, bearing their sheaves with them.

Corks popped as the three friends watched the fun. As Tudor pointed out, you couldn't run from a lion if you didn't know where it was. He had the best part of a bottle of champagne inside him, and felt at least as brave as Hemingway. Roger, as usual, was observing the decadence of middle-class society, unmoved. 'Pity this isn't Clicquot,' was Agard's comment.

Oliver Fry stalked through the mob, still wielding his great mallet. Mona Boylan, with a loaded Winchester, was threatening her section of the crowd with a dose of lead 'if the women and children aren't let through'. The terrified women and children stayed where they were. Sternly

Magda dumped brace after brace of aesthetes in the pond.

The champagne finished, Agard suggested joining the party. 'It's obviously a put-up game of Hilary's.'

'We don't *know*,' said Tudor.

'It's obvious,' Roger said, with adenoidal calm.

'Ah, there's the lion man. Better stick to him,' said Agard.

'Of course.'

'But why?' Tudor wished there had been just one more bottle, or one less Agard.

'Just in case,' Agard said.

'Where is my beautiful lion? Big Johnny, Big Johnny.' Daniel the lion-tamer rushed among the tents, crying for his love. He knew exactly where Big Johnny would be, but he continued to search with great thoroughness in all the wrong places, peering into bushes, declaring his devotion, promising juicy bones.

'Johnny, Johnny, I will tickle you until you laugh. You shall sleep on my own bed. Best neck for breakfast.'

Agard and Tudor and Rashleigh followed him wherever he went.

'If I had my swordstick now,' Agard said.

'The best thing to do,' said Roger, 'is to look the lion straight in the eye.'

'Let's go away.' Tudor tugged their sleeves. 'We don't want to come on the lion suddenly, it might frighten him to death.'

Daniel opened the flaps of the tents of Freaks, crying, 'Bedtime, Johnny,' and saw a dark shape lying on the sawdust. He bent down and raised the shape in his arms. It was the body of a man.

'Mr Byrd, Mr Byrd,' Daniel shouted, 'Mr Byrd is killed.' The sawdust was soaked in blood.

'What did I tell you, what did I tell you. Death over Dymmock,' Tudor whispered.

The three of them looked at the man in Daniel's arms. The upper half of his face was melting. His nose had slipped on to his cheek.

'What's happened to his face? Don't let me look.' Tudor leant forward.

'Big Johnny's mauled him,' Roger said, 'you can see the claw marks.'

Agard brought out his handkerchief and rubbed it across the grotesque face. The nose came off in the handkerchief, the brow began to move slowly upwards, the hair fell from the skull.

'It's Julian Greensleaves,' Tudor said. The entrance to the tent filled with people.

'Is there a doctor in the tent?' Agard asked, removing the last layer of make-up.

A Mr Hartley came shyly towards him from between the legs of the crowd. 'I've got an American degree, please,' he said. 'Honorary, Brown.'

He put his little hand on Greensleaves' pulse, and counted sixty.

'The gentleman is quick,' he cried.

'Give the poor beggar brandy.'

'Who's got some brandy?'

'Emergency only,' Mr Hartley said, and produced from the side-pocket of his morning coat a full-size bottle half-empty.

Agard put the bottle to Greensleaves's lips.

Daniel had disappeared in the confusion, and now he could be heard shouting from outside the tent: 'Everything safe. Come down from the trees. Big Johnny is sleeping in his cage.'

'What's happened? Is Hilary dead?'

'Who killed him?'

'How do you know he was murdered? Careful what you're saying.'

'He's got enough enemies.'

'It isn't Hilary, it's Julian. He tripped over a tent-rope.'

The medical Mr Hartley reassured everyone that his patient was doing well. 'I will issue a bulletin,' he said. 'Now I must go to get my black bag.'

He hurried off towards the midget house, followed by his brothers.

'Where's my black bag, Lennox?'

'In the escritoire.'

'It's full of apples, Constant.'

The crowd watched them go.

A minute later the six Mr Hartleys could be heard screaming in the near distance.

'What the hell's up now?' said Tudor. 'Perhaps the midgets have found another body. Someone looking like me, I shouldn't wonder.'

'Perhaps they've found Hilary again,' Agard said.

They had.

Crammed into the midget house, one foot through the stairs, his head lolling through the window, Hilary Byrd lay smiling with a knife through his throat.